THE JUNIOR GREAT BOOKS

DISCUSSION PROGRAM

JUNIOR GREAT BOOKS

A Program of Interpretive Reading
and Discussion

Series Three, Volume Two

EDITED BY
Richard P. Dennis and Edwin P. Moldof

THE GREAT BOOKS FOUNDATION

© *Copyright 1975 by* **THE GREAT BOOKS FOUNDATION**
Chicago, Illinois

published and distributed by

THE GREAT BOOKS FOUNDATION
*a nonprofit corporation
307 North Michigan Avenue,
Chicago, Illinois 60601*

ACKNOWLEDGMENTS

The Great Books Foundation wishes to thank the following publishers, authors and literary agencies for permission to reprint the material in this Junior Great Books series:

E.P. Dutton & Co., Inc. for "Prince Rabbit," from PRINCE RABBIT AND THE PRINCESS WHO COULD NOT LAUGH, copyright 1966 by A.A. Milne. Illustrated by Mary Shepard. Copyright 1966 by Dorothy Daphne Milne and Spencer Curtis Brown, and "Winnie-the-Pooh," from WINNIE-THE-POOH, copyright 1926 by E.P. Dutton & Co., Inc. Renewal 1954 by A.A. Milne.

Harcourt Brace Jovanovich, Inc. for "Janot Cooks for the Emperor," from THE PIECE OF FIRE, copyright 1942 and 1964 by Harold Courlander.

Henry Holt & Co. for "The Fire on the Mountain," from THE FIRE ON THE MOUNTAIN, copyright 1950 by Harold Courlander & Wolf Leslau.

Holt, Rinehart and Winston, Inc. for "Anansi's Fishing Expedition," and "Kaddo's Wall," from THE COW-TAIL SWITCH AND OTHER WEST AFRICAN STORIES, copyright 1947 by Harold Courlander and George Herzog.

Alfred A. Knopf, for "Little Red Riding Hood" and "The Turnip," from TALES TOLD AGAIN, copyright 1927 and renewed 1955 by Walter de la Mare, and "The Serpent," from OLD NEAPOLITAN FAIRY TALES, copyright 1963 by Rose Laura Mincieli.

Little, Brown and Co. for "The Foolish Man," from ONCE THERE WAS AND ONCE THERE WAS NOT, copyright 1966 by Virginia A. Tashjian.

The Macmillan Company, for "The Fisherman and his Wife," translated from the German by Lucy Crane. Published in 1923 by The Macmillan Company.

David McKay Company, Inc. for "Beauty and the Beast," from THE BLUE FAIRY BOOK by Andrew Lang, Longmans Green, 1948.

Penguin Books, Inc., for "Cinderella," and "The Master Cat Or: Puss-in-Boots," from THE FAIRY TALES OF CHARLES PERRAULT, translated by Geoffrey Brereton.

The Viking Press, Inc. for THE MOUSEWIFE by Rumer Godden, copyright 1951 by Rumer Godden.

CONTENTS

The Serpent   1
Rose Laura Minicieli

Prince Rabbit   13
A.A. Milne

The Foolish Man   33
Virginia A. Tashjian

The Water of Life   39
Jacob and Wilhelm Grimm

The Fire on the Mountain   48
Wolf Leslau and Harold Courlander

Janot Cooks for the Emperor   55
Wolf Leslau and Harold Courlander

Beauty and the Beast   60
Andrew Lang

The Mousewife   87
Rumer Godden

A Short Course on Interpretive Reading, Part Two   101

THE SERPENT

There was once a gardener's wife who longed to have a son more than anything in the world.

It chanced one day that Cola Matteo, her husband, went to the mountain to gather a bundle of faggots. When he came home and opened it he found a pretty little serpent among the twigs. At the sight of this, Sapatella, his wife, heaved a deep sigh and said: "Alas! even the serpents have their little children, but I have none."

At these words, the little serpent spoke and said: "Well then, since you do not have children, take me and you will have made a good bargain, for I shall love you as my mother."

Sapatella, hearing the serpent speaking this way, nearly fainted away, but plucking up courage, she said: "If for nothing else than the affection that you offer me, I am content to take you and care for you." So she fixed a corner of the house for him to live in and gave him food to eat.

The serpent grew from day to day, and when he had grown rather big, he said to Cola Matteo, the gardener: "Listen, my man, I wish to get married."

"With all my heart," said Cola Matteo. "We must look for another serpent like yourself, and try to make a match between you."

"What other serpent are you talking about? It is easy to see that you do not understand. I want the King's daughter to wed; so go and ask the King for her, and tell him it is a serpent who demands her."

Cola Matteo, who was a plain, straightforward kind of man, went innocently to the King and delivered his message. "Know then that a serpent wants your daughter for his wife, and I have come to try to arrange a marriage between them."

The King thought that Cola Matteo was joking and so, in order to get rid of him quickly, he said: "Go and tell the serpent that I will give him my daughter if he turns all the fruit in my orchard into gold." He then burst out laughing and dismissed the gardener.

When Cola Matteo went home, he delivered the answer to the serpent.

"Go tomorrow morning and gather up all the fruit stones you can find in the city, and sow them

The Serpent

in the King's orchard, and you will see pearls strung on rushes," replied the serpent.

So the next morning Cola Matteo took a basket and went from street to street picking up all the stones of peaches, plums, nectarines, apricots, and cherries that he could find. He then went to the orchard of the palace and sowed them as the serpent had instructed him. In an instant the trees shot up, and stems and branches, leaves, flowers, and fruit were all of glittering gold; at the sight of which the King went into an ecstasy of amazement, and cried aloud with joy.

But when Cola Matteo was sent by the serpent to the King to demand the fulfillment of his promise, the King said: "Slowly, slowly, I must first have something else if he would have my daughter. He must pave all the walls and the ground of the orchard with precious stones."

When the gardener told this to the serpent, he said: "Go tomorrow morning and gather up all the bits of broken crockeryware you can find, and throw them on the walks and on the walls of the orchard, for we will not let this small matter stand in our way."

And so, early the next morning, Cola Matteo took a basket under his arm, and went about collecting bits of tiles, lids of crockery pots, pieces of plates and dishes, handles of jugs, spouts of pitchers. He picked up all the spoiled, broken, cracked lamps and all the fragments of pottery he could find in his way. And when he had done all that the serpent had told him, the whole orchard was mantled with emeralds and diamonds, and coated with rubies and sapphires, so that the luster dazzled one's eyes.

The King was struck dumb by this sight and knew not what to make of it. But when the serpent sent again to let him know that he was expecting the fulfillment of his promise, the King answered: "Oh, all that has been done is nothing if he does not turn my whole palace into gold."

When Cola Matteo told the serpent this new fancy of the King's, the serpent said: "Go and gather a bundle of vegetables and rub the bottom of the palace walls with them. We shall see if we can satisfy this whim!"

Away went Cola that very moment and made a great bundle of cabbages, radishes, leeks, parsley, turnips, and carrots; and when he had rubbed the lower part of the palace with it, the walls instantly shone golden as the sun. And when the gardener came again to demand the hand of the Princess, the King was forced this time to call his daughter to him.

The Serpent

And he said, "My dear Grannonia, I have tried to get rid of a suitor who asked to marry you by making such conditions as seemed to me impossible. But as I am beaten and obliged to consent, I pray you, as you are a dutiful daughter, to help me keep my word, and to be content with what fate wills and therefore I must do."

"Do as you please, father," said Grannonia, "for I shall not oppose you." And so the King bade Cola Matteo to tell the serpent to come.

The serpent then set out for the palace, in a coach made all of gold drawn by four golden elephants. Wherever he went the people fled away in terror, seeing such a large and frightful serpent traveling through the city. When he arrived at the palace, the courtiers all trembled like rushes and ran away. Even the very scullions did not dare to stay in the palace. The King and Queen, shivering with fear, crept into a chamber.

Only Grannonia stood her ground, for though her father and her mother cried out: "Fly, fly, Grannonia, save yourself!" she would not stir from the spot, saying: "Why should I fly from the husband you have given me?"

When the serpent came into her room he took Grannonia by the waist with his tail and carried her into another room and fastened the door.

Then shaking off his skin onto the floor as though it had been a cloak, lo and behold! he became a most handsome young Prince with a head covered all over with ringlets of gold.

When the King saw the serpent go into the room with his daughter and shut the door after him, he said to his wife: "Heaven have mercy on her, for that beast will surely kill her."

Then he peeped through the keyhole to see what had become of her. But when he saw the handsome prince, and the skin of the serpent that had been left lying on the ground, the King gave the door a kick. In he rushed and, taking the skin, flung it into the fire and burned it.

When the Prince saw this he cried: "Ah, what have you done? As long as I had that skin I was protected, but now all is lost!" Instantly he turned into a dove and flew out the window, where he struck his head against the panes and cut himself sorely.

Poor Grannonia! She was happy one moment and sad the next. Poor King and Queen! They had meant no harm. But the Princess wept bitterly until far into the night. And when they were all in bed, she took her jewels, which were in her writing desk, and left the palace in search of her Prince.

The Serpent

She went out of the city, guided by the light of the moon; and on her way she met a fox, who asked her if she wished him for company. "By all means, my friend," replied Grannonia. "I should be delighted, for I am not well acquainted with the country." So they traveled along together until they came to a wood. As they were now tired and wished to rest, they sat down under the trees, stretched themselves on the soft grass, and fell asleep.

They did not awaken until early the next morning. After they awoke, they still stayed for some time listening to the songs of the birds, which delighted Grannonia.

When the fox saw how attentively Grannonia was listening to the birds, he said to her: "You would be twice as interested if, like me, you understood what they are saying."

"Please, dear fox, I beg you to tell me what the birds are saying," entreated Grannonia. And when she had coaxed him for some time the fox told her.

"The birds are talking to each other about what has lately befallen a certain King's son who is as beautiful as a jay. Because he had offended a wicked ogress, she had laid him under a spell to pass seven years in the form of a serpent, and when he had nearly ended the seven years, he fell in love with the daughter of a King. One day when he was in a room with the maiden he cast his skin on the ground. Her father seeing the skin rushed in and burned it. Then, when the Prince was flying away in the shape of a dove, he broke a pane in the window to escape. He hurt his head so severely that there is not a doctor in the world who can help him."

Grannonia became very sad, for she knew the Prince to be her own beloved husband. "Tell me, dear fox, is there no cure for him?" she asked.

The fox replied that there was none other than by anointing his wounds with the blood of those very birds that had been telling the story.

When Grannonia heard this, she fell down on her knees to the fox, entreating him to catch those birds for her, that she might get their blood; adding that, like an honest friend, she would reward him when she found her Prince.

"Have patience," said the fox. "Let us wait until night. When the birds have gone to sleep, trust me to climb the tree and capture them, one after another."

So they waited until the end of the day. Then, as soon as the fox saw all the birds fast asleep on the branches, he stole up quietly and one after

The Serpent

another he captured the linnets, larks, blackbirds, woodpeckers, thrushes, jays, flycatchers, little owls, goldfinches, bullfinches, and redbreasts that were on the trees. And when he had killed them all he put the blood in a little bottle.

Grannonia was so overjoyed that she hardly touched the ground with her feet when she walked. But the fox said to her: "Not so fast, my daughter! You have done nothing, unless you mix my blood also with that of the birds." And so saying he set off to run away.

Grannonia immediately saw all her hopes shattered to pieces and quickly she called out to him: "Indeed, fox, there would be some reason for you to save yourself if I were not under so many obligations to you. But you know how much I owe you, so trust me with what I do. Stop and come with me to the city of this King."

The fox never dreamed that he could possibly be outwitted by a woman, so he agreed to travel on with her. But they had hardly gone fifty paces, when she lifted up the stick she carried and gave him such a neat rap on his head that he lay down dead. Then she put his blood into the little bottle and hurried on again until she came to Big Valley, where she went straight to the royal palace. She then sent word to the King that she had come to cure the Prince.

When the King ordered her to be brought before him, he was astonished at seeing a girl undertake a thing that the best doctors in his kingdom had failed to do. However, he thought that no harm could come from trying, so he asked Grannonia to see what she could do.

But Grannonia answered: "If I succeed, you must promise to give him to me for my husband."

The King, who already looked upon his son as dead, answered her: "If you give him to me safe and sound, I will give him to you sound and safe, for it is only fair to give a husband to her that gives me a son."

So they went into the darkened chamber of the Prince, and hardly had she anointed him with the blood than he became well as if nothing had ever ailed him. When Grannonia saw the Prince well and hearty, she bade the King keep his promise.

Whereupon the King turned to his son and said: "My son, a moment ago you were all but dead, and now I see you well again, and can hardly believe it. Therefore, I have promised this maiden that if she cured you she should have you for her husband. Enable me now to perform my promise by all the love you bear me, since gratitude obliges me to pay this debt."

The Serpent

When the Prince heard these words, he said: "Sir, I would that I were free to prove to you the love I bear you. But as I have already pledged my faith to another woman, you would not consent that I should break my word. Nor would this maiden wish that I should do such a wrong to her whom I love, nor can I change my mind."

When Grannonia heard this, she felt a secret pleasure at finding herself still alive in the memory of the Prince. Her whole face became crimson as she said: "If I could induce this other maiden to resign her claims, would you then consent to my wish?"

"Never," replied the Prince, "will I forget the image of her whom I love. I shall ever remain of the same mind and will, and I would sooner be dead than play so mean a trick!"

Grannonia could no longer contain herself. She asked that the curtains be drawn from the window, for the chamber was still darkened and the Prince had not recognized her.

The Prince now realized who Grannonia really was and he embraced her with joy. He told his father what had happened to him and what he had suffered for his love.

Then they sent messengers to invite her parents, the King and Queen of Long Field, and they celebrated the wedding with a wonderful feast. And so the Prince and Princess lived happily together for many a year.

PRINCE RABBIT

Once upon a time there was a King who had no children. Sometimes he would say to the Queen, "If only we had a son!" and the Queen would answer, "If only we had!" Another day he would say, "If only we had a daughter!" and the Queen would sigh and answer, "Yes, even if we had a daughter, that would be something." But they had no children at all.

As the years went on, and there were still no children in the Royal palace, the people began to ask each other who would be the next King to reign over them. And some said that perhaps it would be the Chancellor, which was a pity, as nobody liked him very much; and others said that there would be no King at all, but that everybody would be equal. Those who were lowest of all thought that this would be a satisfactory ending of the matter, but those who were higher up felt that, though in some respects it would be a good thing, yet in other respects it would be an ill-advised state of affairs; and they hoped, therefore, that a young

Prince would be born in the palace. But no Prince was born.

One day, when the Chancellor was in audience with the King, it seemed well to him to speak what was in the people's minds.

"Your Majesty," he said, and then stopped, wondering how best to put it.

"Well?" said the King.

"Have I Your Majesty's permission to speak my mind?"

"So far, yes," said the King.

Encouraged by this, the Chancellor resolved to put the matter plainly. "In the event of Your Majesty's death—" He coughed and began again. "If Your Majesty ever *should* die," he said, "which in any case will not be for many years—if ever—as, I need hardly say, Your Majesty's loyal subjects earnestly hope—I mean they hope it will be never. But assuming for the moment—making the sad assumption—"

"You said you wanted to speak your mind," interrupted the King. "Is this it?"

"Yes, Your Majesty."

"Then I don't think much of it."

"Thank you, Your Majesty."

"What you are trying to say is, 'Who will be the next King?' "

"Quite so, Your Majesty."

"Ah!" The King was silent for a little. Then he said, "I can tell you who won't be."

The Chancellor did not seek for information on this point, feeling that in the circumstances the answer was obvious.

"What do you suggest yourself?"

"That Your Majesty choose a successor from among the young and the highly born of the country, putting him to whatever test seems good to Your Majesty."

The King pulled at his beard and frowned. "There must be not one test, but many tests. Let all who will offer themselves, provided only that that they are under the age of twenty and wellborn. See to it."

He waved his hand in dismissal, and with an accuracy established by long practice the Chancellor retired backward out of the palace.

On the following morning, therefore, it was announced that all those who were ambitious to be appointed the King's successor, and who were of high birth and not yet come to the age of twenty, should present themselves a week later for the tests to which His Majesty desired to put them, the first of which would be a running race. Whereat the people rejoiced, for they wished to be ruled by one to whom they could look up, and running was much esteemed in that country.

On the appointed day the excitement was great. All along the course, which was once around the castle, large crowds were massed, and at the finishing point the King and Queen themselves were seated in a specially erected pavilion. And to this the competitors were brought to be introduced to Their Majesties. There were nine young nobles, well-built and handsome and (it was thought) intelligent, who were competitors. And there was also one Rabbit.

The Chancellor had first noticed the Rabbit when he was lining up the competitors, pinning numbers on their backs so that the people should identify them, and giving them such instructions as seemed necessary to him. "Now, now, be off with you," he said. "Competitors only, this way." And he made a motion of impatient dismissal with his foot.

"I *am* a competitor," said the Rabbit. "And I don't think it is usual," he added with dignity, "for the starter to kick one of the competitors just at the beginning of an important race. It looks like favoritism."

"*You* can't be a competitor," laughed all the nobles.

"Why not? Read the rules."

The Chancellor, feeling rather hot suddenly, read the rules. The Rabbit was certainly under twenty; he had a pedigree which showed that he was of the highest birth; and—

"And," said the Rabbit, "I am ambitious to be appointed the King's successor. Those were all the conditions. Now let's get on with the race."

But first came the introduction to the King. One by one the competitors came up...and at the end—

"This," said the Chancellor, as airily as he could, "is Rabbit."

Rabbit bowed in the most graceful manner possible, first to the King and then to the Queen. But the King only stared at him. Then he turned to the Chancellor.

"Well?"

The Chancellor shrugged his shoulders. "His entry does not appear to lack validity," he said.

"He means, Your Majesty, that it is all right," explained Rabbit.

The King laughed suddenly. "Go on," he said. "We can always have a race for a new Chancellor afterward."

So the race was started. And the young Lord Calomel was much cheered on coming in second, not only by Their Majesties, but also by Rabbit, who had finished the course some time before and was now lounging in the Royal pavilion.

"A very good style, Your Majesty," said Rabbit, turning to the King. "Altogether he seems to be a most promising youth."

"Most," said the King grimly. "So much so that I do not propose to trouble the rest of the competitors. The next test shall take place between you and him."

"Not racing again, please, Your Majesty. That would hardly be fair to His Lordship."

"No, not racing. Fighting."

"Ah! What sort of fighting?"

"With swords," said the King.

"I am a little rusty with swords, but I daresay in a day or two—"

"It will be now," said the King.

"You mean, Your Majesty, as soon as Lord Calomel has recovered his breath?"

The King answered nothing, but turned to his Chancellor. "Tell the young Lord Calomel that in half an hour I desire him to fight with this Rabbit—"

"The young Lord Rabbit," murmured the other competitor to the Chancellor.

"To fight with him for my kingdom."

Prince Rabbit

"*And* borrow me a sword, will you?" said the Rabbit. "Quite a small one. I don't want to hurt him."

So, half an hour later, on a level patch of grass in front of the pavilion, the fight began. It was a short but exciting struggle. Calomel, whirling his long sword in his strong right arm, dashed upon Rabbit, and Rabbit, carrying his short sword in his teeth, dodged between Calomel's legs and brought him toppling. And when it was seen that the young lord rose from the ground with a broken arm, and that with the utmost gallantry he had now taken his sword in his left hand, the people cheered. And Rabbit, dropping his sword for a moment, cheered too; and then he picked it up and got it entangled in his adversary's legs again, so that again the young Lord Calomel crashed to the ground, this time with a sprained ankle. And there he lay.

Rabbit trotted into the Royal pavilion and dropped his sword in the Chancellor's lap. "Thank you so much," he said. "Have I won?" And the King frowned and pulled at his beard. "There are other tests," he muttered.

But what were they to be? It was plain that Lord Calomel was in no condition for another physical test. What, then, of an intellectual test?

"After all," said the King to the Queen that night, "intelligence is a quality not without value in a ruler."

"Is it?" asked the Queen doubtfully.

"I have found it so," said the King, a trifle haughtily.

"Oh," said the Queen.

"There is a riddle of which my father was fond, the answer to which has never been revealed save to the Royal House. We might make this the final test between them."

"What is the riddle?"

"I fancy it goes like this." He thought for a moment and then recited it, beating time with his hand.

> "*My* first *I do for your delight,*
> *Although 'tis neither black nor white.*
> *My* second *looks the other way,*
> *Yet always goes to bed by day.*
> *My* whole *can fly and climb a tree,*
> *And sometimes swims upon the sea.*"

"What is the answer?" asked the Queen.

"As far as I remember," said His Majesty, "it is either *Dormouse* or *Raspberry*."

"*Dormouse* doesn't make sense," objected the Queen.

Prince Rabbit

"Neither does *Raspberry*," pointed out the King.

"Then how can they guess it?"

"They can't. But my idea is that young Calomel should be secretly told beforehand what the answer is, so that he may win the competition."

"Is that fair?" asked the Queen doubtfully.

"Yes," said the King. "Certainly. Or I wouldn't have suggested it."

So it was duly announced by the Chancellor that the final test between the young Lord Calomel and Rabbit would be the solving of an ancient riddle-me-ree which in the past had baffled all save those of Royal blood. Copies of the riddle had been sent to the competitors, and in a week from that day they would be called upon to give their answers before Their Majesties and the full court. And with Lord Calomel's copy went a message, which said this:

"*From a Friend.* The answer is *Dormouse.* BURN THIS."

The day came around; and Calomel and Rabbit were brought before Their Majesties; and they bowed to Their Majesties and were ordered to be seated, for Calomel's ankle was still painful to him. And when the Chancellor had called for silence, the King addressed those present, explaining the conditions of the test to them.

"And the answer to the riddle," he said, "is in this sealed paper, which I now hand to my Chancellor, in order that he shall open it as soon as the competitors have told us what they know of the matter."

The people, being uncertain what else to do, cheered slightly.

"I will ask Lord Calomel first," His Majesty went on. He looked at His Lordship, and His Lordship nodded slightly. And Rabbit, noticing that nod, smiled suddenly to himself.

The young Lord Calomel tried to look very wise, and he said, "There are many possible answers to this riddle-me-ree, but the best answer seems to me to be *Dormouse*."

"Let someone take a note of that answer," said the King: whereupon the chief secretary wrote down: "LORD CALOMEL—*Dormouse*."

"Now," said the King to Rabbit, "what suggestion have you to make in this matter?"

Rabbit, who had spent an anxious week inventing answers each more impossible than the last, looked down modestly.

"Well?" said the King.

"Your Majesty," said the Rabbit with some

apparent hesitation, "I have a great respect for the intelligence of the young Lord Calomel, but I think that in this matter he is mistaken. The answer is not, as he suggests, *Wood-louse*, but *Dormouse*."

"I *said Dormouse*," cried Calomel indignantly.

"I thought you said *Wood-louse*," said the Rabbit in surprise.

"He certainly said *Dormouse*," said the King coldly.

"*Wood-louse*, I *think*," said Rabbit.

" 'LORD CALOMEL—*Dormouse*,' " read out the chief secretary.

"There you are," said Calomel. "I did say *Dormouse*."

"My apologies," said Rabbit, with a bow. "Then we are both right, for *Dormouse* it certainly is."

The Chancellor broke open the sealed paper and, to the amazement of nearly all present, read out, "*Dormouse*... Apparently, Your Majesty," he said in some surprise, "they are both equally correct."

The King scowled. In some way which he didn't quite understand, he had been tricked.

"May I suggest, Your Majesty," the Chancellor went on, "that they be asked now some question of a different order, such as can be answered, after not more than a few minutes' thought, here in Your Majesty's presence? Some problem in the higher mathematics, for instance, such as might be profitable for a future King to know."

"What question?" asked His Majesty, a little nervously.

"Well, as an example—what is seven times six?" And behind his hand he whispered to the King, "Forty-two."

Not a muscle of the King's face moved, but he looked thoughtfully at the Lord Calomel. Supposing His Lordship did not know!

"Well?" he said reluctantly. "What is the answer?"

The young Lord Calomel thought for some time and then said, "Fifty-four."

"And you?" said the King to the Rabbit.

Rabbit wondered what to say. As long as he gave the same answers as Calomel, he could not lose in the encounter, yet in this case "forty-two" was the right answer. But the King, who could do no wrong, even in arithmetic, might decide, for the purposes of the competition, that "fifty-four" was an answer more becoming to the future ruler of the country. Was it, then, safe to say "forty-two"?

"Your Majesty," he said, "there are several possible answers to this extraordinary novel conundrum. At first sight the obvious solution would appear to be 'forty-two.' The objection to this solution is that is lacks originality. I have long felt that a progressive country such as ours might well strike out a new line in the matter. Let us agree that in future seven sixes are fifty-four. In that case the answer, as Lord Calomel has pointed out, *is* 'fifty-four.' But if Your Majesty would prefer to cling to the old style of counting, then Your Majesty and Your Majesty's Chancellor would make the answer 'forty-two.' "

After saying which, Rabbit bowed gracefully, both to Their Majesties and to his opponent and sat down again.

The King scratched his head in a puzzled sort of way. "The correct answer," he said, "is, or will be in the future, 'fifty-four.' "

"Make a note of that," whispered the Chancellor to the chief secretary.

"Lord Calomel guessed this at his first attempt; Rabbit at his second attempt. I therefore declare Lord Calomel the winner."

"Shame!" said Rabbit.

"Who said that?" cried the King furiously.

Rabbit looked over his shoulder with the object of identifying the culprit, but was apparently unsuccessful.

"However," went on the King, "in order that there should be no doubt in the minds of my people as to the absolute fairness with which this competition is being conducted, there will be one further test. It happens that a King is often called upon to make speeches and exhortations to his people, and for this purpose the ability to stand evenly upon two legs for a considerable length of time is of much value to him. The next test, therefore, will be—"

But at this point Lord Calomel cleared his throat so loudly that the King had to stop and listen to him.

"Quite so," said the King. "The next test, therefore, will be held in a month's time, when His Lordship's ankle is healed, and it will be a test to see who can balance himself longest upon two legs only."

Rabbit lolloped back to his home in the wood, pondering deeply.

Now, there was an enchanter who lived in the wood, a man of many magical gifts. He could (it was averred by the countryside) extract colored ribbons from his mouth, cook plum puddings in a hat, and produce as many as ten silk handkerchiefs, knotted together, from a twist of paper. And that night, after a simple dinner of salad, Rabbit called upon him.

"Can you," he said, "turn a rabbit into a man?"

The enchanter considered this carefully. "I can," he said at last, "turn a plum pudding into a rabbit."

"That," said Rabbit, "to be frank, would not be a helpful operation."

"I can turn almost anything into a rabbit," said the enchanter with growing enthusiasm. "In fact, I like doing it."

Then Rabbit had an idea. "Can you turn a man into a rabbit?"

"I did once. At least, I turned a baby into a baby rabbit."

"When was that?"

"Eighteen years ago. At the court of King Nicodemus. I was giving an exhibition of my powers to him and his good Queen. I asked one of the company to lend me a baby, never thinking for a moment that—The young Prince was handed up. I put a red silk handkerchief over him and waved my hands. Then I took the handkerchief away .... The Queen was very distressed. I tried everything I could, but it was useless. The King was most generous about it. He said that I could keep the rabbit. I carried it about with me for some weeks, but one day it escaped. Dear, dear!" he wiped his eyes gently with a red silk handkerchief.

"Most interesting," said Rabbit, "Well, this is what I want you to do." And they discussed the matter from the beginning.

A month later the great standing competition was to take place. When all was ready, the King rose to make his opening remarks.

"We are now," he began, "to make one of the most interesting tests between our two candidates for the throne. At the word 'Go!' they will—" and then he stopped suddenly. "Why, what's this?" he said, putting on his spectacles. "Where is the young Lord Calomel? And what is that second rabbit doing? There was no need to bring your brother," he added severely to Rabbit.

"I am Lord Calomel," said the second rabbit meekly.

"Oh!" said the King.

"Go!" said the Chancellor, who was a little deaf.

Rabbit, who had been practicing for a month, jumped on his back paws and remained there.

Prince Rabbit

Lord Calomel, who had had no practice at all, remained on all fours. In the crowd at the back the enchanter chuckled to himself.

"How long do I stay like this?" asked Rabbit.

"This is all very awkward and distressing," said the King.

"May I get down?" said Rabbit.

"There is no doubt that the Rabbit has won," said the Chancellor.

"Which rabbit?" cried the King crossly. "They're both rabbits."

"The one with the white spots behind the ears," said Rabbit helpfully. "May I get down?"

There was a sudden cry from the back of the hall. "Your Majesty?"

"Well, well, what is it?"

The enchanter pushed his way forward. "May I look, Your Majesty?" he said in a trembling voice. "White spots behind the ears? Dear, dear! Allow me!" He seized Rabbit's ears and bent them this way and that.

"Ow!" said Rabbit.

"It is! Your Majesty, it is!"

"Is what?"

"The son of the late King Nicodemus, whose country is now joined to your own. Prince Silvio."

"Quite so," said Rabbit airily, hiding his

surprise. "Didn't any of your recognize me?"

"Nicodemus only had one son," said the Chancellor, "and he died as a baby."

"Not died," said the enchanter, and forthwith explained the whole sad story.

"I see," said the King, when the story was ended. "But of course that is neither here nor there. A competition like this must be conducted with absolute impartiality." He turned to the Chancellor. "Which of them won that last test?"

"Prince Silvio," said the Chancellor.

"Then, my dear Prince Silvio—"

"One moment," interrupted the enchanter excitedly. "I've just thought of the words. I *knew* there were some words you had to say."

He threw his red silk handkerchief over Rabbit and cried, "Hey presto!"

And the handkerchief rose and rose and rose....And there was Prince Silvio!

You can imagine how loudly the people cheered. But the King appeared not to notice that anything surprising had happened.

"Then, my dear Prince Silvio," he went on, "as the winner of this most interesting series of contests, you are appointed successor to our throne."

"Your Majesty," said Silvio, "this is too

much." And he turned to the enchanter and said, "My I borrow your handkerchief for a moment? My emotion has overcome me."

So on the following day Prince Rabbit was duly proclaimed heir to the throne before all the people. But not until the ceremony was over did he return the enchanter's red handkerchief.

"And now," he said to the enchanter, "you may restore Lord Calomel to his proper shape."

And the enchanter placed his handkerchief on Lord Calomel's head and said, "Hey presto!" and Lord Calomel stretched himself and said, "Thanks very much." But he said it rather coldly, as if he were not really very grateful.

So they all lived happily for a long time. And Prince Rabbit married the most beautiful Princess of those parts, and when a son was born to them there was much feasting and jollification. And the King gave a great party, whereat minstrels, tumblers, jugglers and suchlike were present in large quantities to give pleasure to the company. But, in spite of a suggestion made by the Princess, the enchanter was not present.

"But I hear he is so clever," said the Princess to her husband.

"He has many amusing inventions," replied the Prince, "but some of them are not in the best of taste."

"Very well, dear," said the Princess.

THE FOOLISH MAN

Once there was and was not in ancient Armenia a poor man who worked and toiled hard from morn till night, but nevertheless remained poor.

Finally one day he became so discouraged that he decided to go in search of God in order to ask Him how long he must endure such poverty—and to beg of Him a favor.

On his way, the man met a wolf.

"Good day, brother man," asked the wolf. "Where are you bound in such a hurry?"

"I go in search of God," replied the man. "I have a complaint to lodge with Him."

"Well," said the wolf, "would you do me a kindness? When you find God, will you complain to Him for me, too? Tell Him you met a half-starved wolf who searches the woods and fields for food from morning till night—and though he works hard and long, still finds nothing to eat. Ask God why He does not provide for wolves since He created them?"

"I will tell Him of your complaint," agreed the

poor man, and continued on his way.

As he hurried over the hills and through the valleys, he chanced to meet a beautiful maid.

"Where do you go in such a hurry, my brother?" asked the maid.

"I go in search of God," replied the man.

"Oh, kind friend, when you find God, would you ask Him something for me? Tell Him you met a maid on your way. Tell Him she is young and fair and very rich—but very unhappy. Ask God why she cannot know happiness. What will become of her? Ask God why He will not help her to be happy."

"I will tell Him of your trouble," promised the poor man, and continued on his way.

Soon he met a tree which seemed all dried up and dying even though it grew by the side of a river.

"Where do you go in such a hurry, O traveler?" called the dry tree.

"I go in search of God," answered the man. "I have a complaint to lodge with Him."

"Wait a moment, O traveler," begged the tree, "I, too, have a question for God.

"Please ask Him why I am dry both in summer and winter. Though I live by this wet river, my leaves do not turn green. Ask God how long I must suffer. Ask Him that for me, good friend," said the tree.

The man listened to the tree's complaint, promised to tell God, and continued once again upon his way.

Finally, the poor man reached the end of his journey. He found God seated beneath the ledge of a cliff.

"Good day," said the man as he approached God.

"Welcome, traveler," God returned his greeting. "Why have you journeyed so far? What is your trouble?"

"Well, I want to know why there is injustice in the world. Is it fair that I toil and labor from morn till night—yet never seem to earn enough for a full stomach, while many who do not work half as hard as I live and eat as rich men do?"

"Go then," replied God. "I present you the Gift of Luck. Go find it and enjoy it to the end of your days."

"I have yet another complaint, my Lord," continued the man—and he proceeded to list the complaints and requests of the starved wolf, the beautiful maid, and the parched tree.

God gave appropriate answers to each of the three complaints, whereupon the poor man thanked Him and started on his way homeward.

Soon he came upon the dry, parched tree.

"What message did God have for me?" asked the tree.

"He said that beneath your trunk there lies a pot of gold which prevents the water from seeping up your trunk to your leaves. God said your branches will never turn green until the pot of gold is removed."

"Well, what are you waiting for, foolish man!" exclaimed the tree. "Dig up that pot of gold. It will make you rich—and permit me to turn green and live again!"

"Oh, no," protested the man. "I have no time to dig up a pot of gold. God has given me the Gift of Luck. I must hurry and search for it." And he hurried on his way.

Presently, he met the beautiful maid who was waiting for him. "Oh, kind friend, what message did God have for me?"

"God said that you will soon meet a kind man who will prove to be a good life's companion to you. No longer will you be lonely. Happiness and contentment will come to you," reported the poor man.

"In that case, what are you waiting for, foolish man?" exclaimed the maid. "Why don't you stay

The Foolish Man

here and be my life's companion."

"Oh, no! I have no time to stay with you. God has given me the Gift of Luck. I must hurry and search for it." And the man hurried on his way.

Some distance away, the starving wolf impatiently awaited the man's coming, and hailed him with a shout.

"Well, what did God say? What message did He send to me?"

"Brother wolf, so many things have happened since I saw you last," said the man. "I hardly know where to begin. On my way to seek God, I met a beautiful maid who begged me to ask God the reason for her unhappiness. And I met a parched tree who wanted God to explain the dryness of its branches even though it stood by a wet river.

"I told God about these matters. He bade me tell the maid to seek a life's companion in order to find happiness. He bade me warn the tree about a pot of gold buried near its trunk which must be removed before the branches can recieve nourishment from the earth.

"On my return, I brought God's answers to the maid and to the tree. The maid asked me to stay and be her life's companion, while the tree asked me to dig up the pot of gold.

"Of course, I had to refuse both since God gave me the Gift of Luck—and I must hurry along to search for it!"

"Ah-h-h, brother man, and what was God's reply to me?" asked the starving wolf.

"As for you," replied the man, "God said that you would remain hungry until you met a silly and foolish man whom you could eat up. Only then, said God, would your hunger be satisfied."

"Hmmmmmm," mused the wolf, "where in the world will I find a man more silly and stupid than you?"

And he ate up the foolish man.

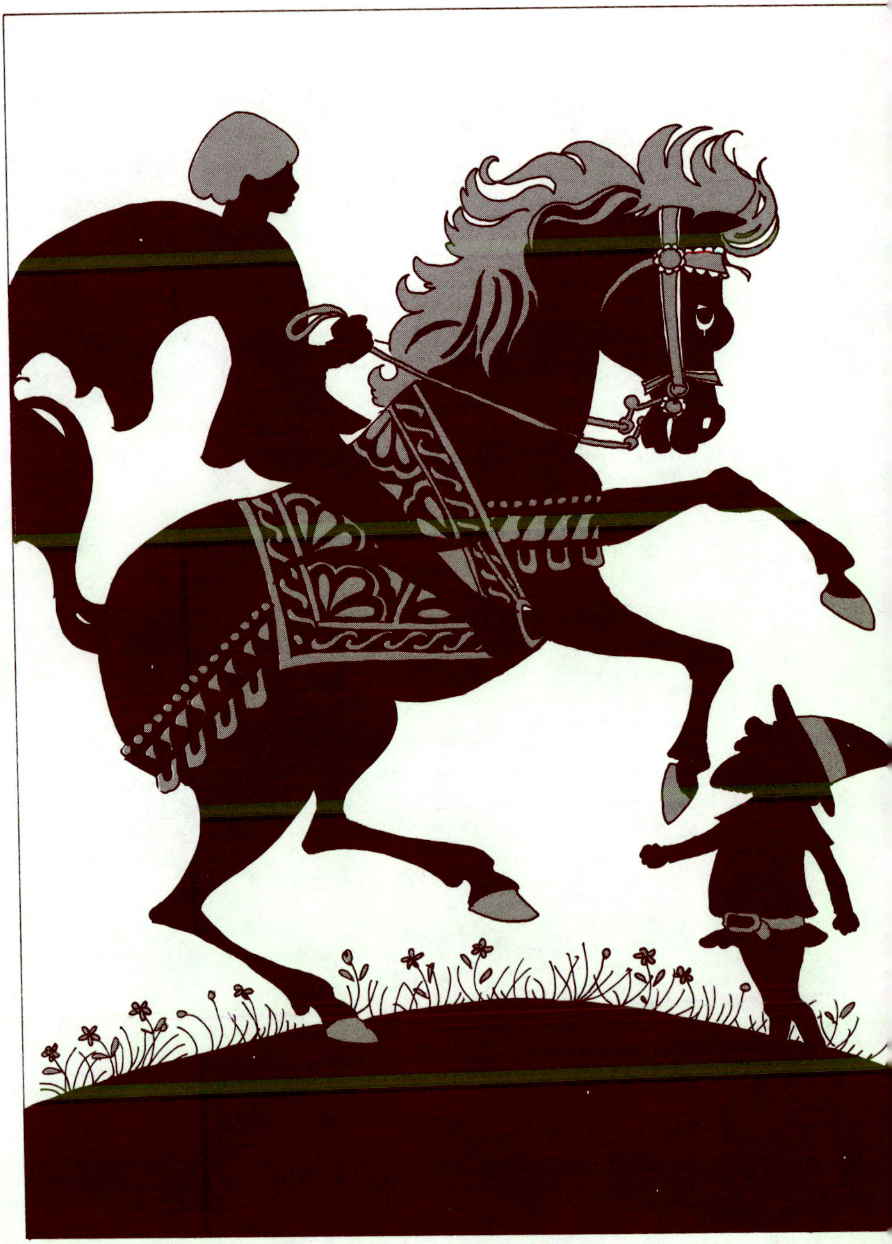

THE WATER OF LIFE

THERE WAS once a King who had an illness, and no one believed that he would come out of it with his life. He had three sons who were much distressed about it, and went down into the palace garden and wept. There they met an old man who inquired as to the cause of their grief. They told him that their father was so ill that he would most certainly die, for nothing seemed to cure him. Then the old man said, "I know of one more remedy, and that is the water of life; if he drinks of it he will become well again; but it is hard to find." The eldest said, "I will manage to find it," and went to the sick King, and begged to be allowed to go forth in search of the water of life, for that alone could save him. "No," said the King, "the danger of it is too great. I would rather die." But he begged so long that the King consented. The prince thought in his heart, "If I bring the water, then I shall be best beloved of my father, and shall inherit the kingdom." So he set out, and when he had ridden forth a little distance, a dwarf stood there in the road who called to him and said, "Whither away so fast?" "Silly shrimp," said the prince, very haughtily, "it is nothing to you," and rode on. But the little dwarf had grown angry, and had wished an evil wish. Soon after this the prince entered a ravine, and the further he rode the closer the mountains drew together, and at last the road became so narrow that he could not advance a step further; it was impossible either to turn his horse or to dismount from the saddle, and he was shut in there as if in prison. The sick King waited long for him, but he came not. Then the second son said, "Father, let me go forth to seek the water," and thought to himself, "If my brother is dead, then the kingdom will fall to me." At first the King would not allow him to go either, but at last he yielded, so the prince set out on the same road that his brother had taken, and he too met the dwarf, who stopped him to ask, whither he was going in such haste? "Little shrimp," said the prince, "that is nothing to you," and rode on without giving him another look. But the dwarf bewitched him, and he, like the other, got into a ravine, and could neither go forward nor backward. So fare haughty people.

As the second son also remained away, the youngest begged to be allowed to go forth to fetch the water, and at last the King was obliged to let

The Water of Life

him go. When he met the dwarf and the latter asked him whither he was going in such haste, he stopped, gave him an explanation, and said, "I am seeking the water of life, for my father is sick unto death." "Do you know, then, where that is to be found?" "No," said the prince. "As you have borne yourself as is seemly, and not haughtily like your false brothers, I will give you the information and tell you how you may obtain the water of life. It springs from a fountain in the courtyard of an enchanted castle, but you will not be able to make your way to it, if I do not give you an iron wand and two small loaves of bread. Strike thrice with the wand on the iron door of the castle, and it will spring open: inside lie two lions with gaping jaws, but if you throw a loaf to each of them, they will be quieted, then hasten to fetch some of the water of life before the clock strikes twelve, else the door will shut again, and you will be imprisoned." The prince thanked him, took the wand and the bread, and set out on his way. When he arrived, everything was as the dwarf had said. The door sprang open at the third stroke of the wand, and when he had appeased the lions with the bread, he entered into the castle, and came in a large and splendid hall, wherein sat some enchanted princes whose rings he drew off their fingers. A sword and a loaf of bread were lying there, which he carried away. After this, he entered a chamber, in which was a beautiful maiden who rejoiced when she saw him, kissed him, and told him that he had delivered her, and should have the whole of her kingdom, and that if he would return in a year their wedding should be celebrated; likewise she told him where the spring of the water of life was, and that he was to hasten and draw some of it before the clock struck twelve. Then he went onward, and at last entered a room where there was a beautiful newly made bed, and as he was very weary, he felt inclined to rest a little. So he lay down and fell asleep. When he awoke, it was striking a quarter to twelve. He sprang up in a fright, ran to the spring, drew some water in a cup which stood near, and hastened away. But just as he was passing through the iron door, the clock struck twelve, and the door fell to with such violence that it carried away a piece of his heel. He, however, rejoicing at having obtained the water of life, went homeward, and again passed the dwarf. When the latter saw the sword and the loaf, he said, "With these you have won great wealth; with the sword you can slay whole armies, and the bread will never come to an end." But the prince would not go home to his father without his brothers, and said, "Dear dwarf, can you not tell me where my two brothers

The Water of Life

are? They went out before I did in search of the water of life, and have not returned." "They are imprisoned between two mountains," said the dwarf. "I have condemned them to stay there, because they were so haughty." Then the prince begged until the dwarf released them; he warned him, however, and said, "Beware of them, for they have bad hearts." When his brothers came, he rejoiced, and told them how things had gone with him, that he had found the water of life, and had brought a cupful away with him, and had delivered a beautiful princess, who was willing to wait a year for him, and then their wedding was to be celebrated, and he would obtain a great kingdom. After that they rode on together, and chanced upon a land where war and famine reigned, and the King already thought he must perish, for the scarcity was so great. Then the prince went to him and gave him the loaf, wherewith he fed and satisfied the whole of his kingdom, and then the prince gave him the sword also, wherewith he slew the hosts of his enemies, and could now live in rest and peace. The prince then took back his loaf and his sword, and the three brothers rode on. But after this they entered two more countries where war and famine reigned, and each time the prince gave his loaf and his sword to the Kings, and had now delivered three kingdoms, and after that they went on board a ship and sailed over the sea. During the passage, the two eldest conversed apart and said, "The youngest has found the water of life and not we, for that our father will give him the kingdom—the kingdom which belongs to us, and he will rob us of all our fortune." They then began to seek revenge, and plotted with each other to destroy him. They waited until once when they found him fast asleep, then they poured the water of life out of the cup, and took it for themselves, but into the cup they poured salt sea-water. Now therefore, when they arrived at home, the youngest took his cup to the sick King in order that he might drink out of it, and be cured. But scarcely had he drunk a very little of the salt sea-water than he became still worse than before. And as he was lamenting over this, the two eldest brothers came, and accused the youngest of having intended to poison him, and said that they had brought him the true water of life, and handed it to him. He had scarcely tasted it, when he felt his sickness departing, and became strong and healthy as in the days of his youth. After that they both went to the youngest, mocked him, and said, "You certainly found the water of life, but you have had the pain, and we the gain; you should have been sharper, and should have kept your eyes open. We took it from you while you were asleep at sea, and when a year is over, one of us will go and fetch the beautiful princess. But beware that you do not disclose any of this to our father; indeed he does not trust you, and if you say a single word, you shall lose your life into the bargain, but if you keep silent, you shall have it as a gift."

The old King was angry with his youngest son, and thought he had plotted against his life. So he summoned the court together, and had sentence pronounced upon his son, that he should be secretly shot. And once when the prince was riding forth to the chase, suspecting no evil, the King's huntsman had to go with him, and when they were quite alone in the forest, the huntsman looked so sorrowful that the prince said to him, "Dear huntsman, what ails you?" The huntsman said, "I cannot tell you, and yet I ought." Then the prince said, "Say openly what it is, I will pardon you." "Alas!" said the huntsman, "I am to shoot you dead, the King has ordered me to do it." Then the prince was shocked, and said, "Dear huntsman, let me live; there, I give you my royal garments; give me your common ones in their stead." The huntsman said, "I will willingly do that, indeed I should not have been able to shoot you." Then they exchanged clothes, and the huntsman returned home; the prince, however, went further into the forest. After a time three wagons of gold and precious stones came to the King for his youngest son, which were sent by the three Kings who had slain their enemies with the prince's sword, and maintained their people with his bread, and who wished to show their gratitude for it. The old King then thought, "Can my son have been innocent?" and said to his people, "Would that he were still alive, how it grieves me that I have suffered him to be killed!" "He still lives," said the huntsman, "I could not find it in my heart to carry out your command," and told the King how it had happened. Then a stone fell from the King's heart, and he had it proclaimed in every country that his son might return and be taken into favor again.

The princess, however, had a road made up to her palace which was quite bright and golden, and told her people that whoever came riding straight along it to her, would be the right suitor and was to be admitted, and whoever rode by the side of it, was not the right one, and was not to be admitted. As the time was now close at hand, the eldest thought he would hasten to go to the King's daughter, and give himself out as her deliverer, and thus win her for his bride, and the kingdom to boot. Therefore he rode forth, and when he arrived in front of the palace, and saw the splendid golden road, he thought it would be a sin and a shame if he were to ride over that, and turned aside, and rode on the right side of it. But when he came to the door, the servants told him that he was not the right man, and was to go away again. Soon after this the second prince set out, and when he came to the golden road, and his horse had put one foot on it, he thought it would be a sin and a shame to tread a piece of it off, and he turned aside and rode on the left side of it, and when he reached the door, the attendants told him he was not the right one, and was to go away again. When at last the year had entirely expired, the third son likewise wished to ride out of the forest to his beloved, with her to forget his sorrows. So he set out and thought of her so incessantly, and wished to be with her so much, that he never noticed the golden road at all. So his horse rode onward up the middle of it, and when he came to the door, it was opened and the princess received him with joy, and said he was her deliverer, and lord of the kingdom, and their wedding was celebrated with great rejoicing. When it was over she told him that his father invited him to come to him, and had forgiven him. So he rode thither, and told him everything; how his brothers had betrayed him, and how he had nevertheless kept silence. The old King wished to punish them, but they had put to sea, and never came back as long as they lived.

THE FIRE ON THE MOUNTAIN

People say that in the old days in the city of Addis Ababa there was a young man by the name of Arha. He had come as a boy from the country of Guragé, and in the city he became the servant of a rich merchant, Haptom Hasei.

Haptom Hasei was so rich that he owned everything that money could buy, and often he was very bored because he had tired of everything he knew, and there was nothing new for him to do.

One cold night, when the damp wind was blowing across the plateau, Haptom called to Arha to bring wood for the fire. When Arha was finished, Haptom began to talk.

"How much cold can a man stand?" he said, speaking at first to himself. "I wonder if it would be possible for a man to stand on the highest peak, Mount Sululta, where the coldest winds blow, through an entire night without blankets or clothing and yet not die?"

"I don't know," Arha said. "But wouldn't it be

"The Fire on the Mountain," from THE FIRE ON THE MOUNTAIN, copyright 1950 by Harold Courlander and Wolf Leslau. Reprinted by permission of Henry Holt & Co.

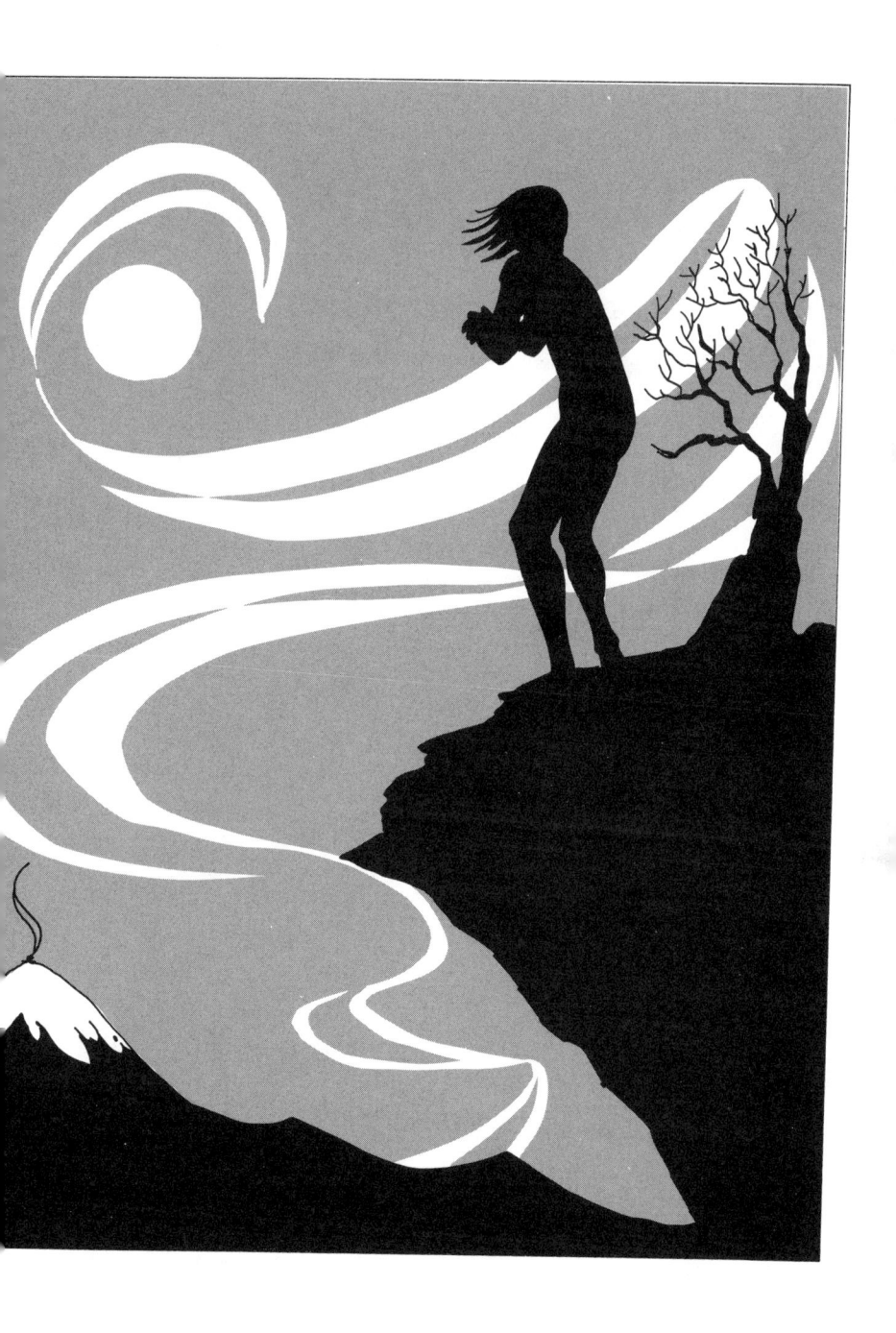

The Fire on the Mountain

a foolish thing?"

"Perhaps, if he had nothing to gain by it, it would be a foolish thing to spend the night that way," Haptom said. "But I would be willing to bet that a man couldn't do it."

"I am sure a courageous man could stand naked on Mount Sululta throughout an entire night and not die of it," Arha said. "But as for me, it isn't my affair since I've nothing to bet."

"Well, I'll tell you what," Haptom said. "Since you are so sure it can be done, I'll make a bet with you anyway. If you can stand among the rocks on Mount Sululta for an entire night without food or water, or clothing or blankets or fire, and not die of it, then I will give you ten acres of good farmland for your own, with a house and cattle."

Arha could hardly believe what he had heard.

"Do you really mean this?" he asked.

"I am a man of my word," Haptom replied.

"Then tomorrow night I will do it," Arha said, "and afterwards, for all the years to come, I shall till my own soil."

But he was very worried, because the wind swept bitterly across that peak. So in the morning Arha went to a wise old man from the Guragé tribe and told him of the bet he had made. The old man listened quietly and thoughtfully, and when Arha had finished he said:

"I will help you. Across the valley from Sululta is a high rock which can be seen in the daytime. Tomorrow night as the sun goes down, I shall build a fire there, so that it can be seen from where you stand on the peak. All night long you must watch the light of my fire. Do not close your eyes or let the darkness creep upon you. As you watch my fire, think of its warmth, and think of me, your friend, sitting there tending it for you. If you do this you will survive, no matter how bitter the night wind."

Arha thanked the old man warmly and went back to Haptom's house with a light heart. He told Haptom he was ready, and in the afternoon Haptom sent him, under the watchful eyes of other servants, to the top of Mount Sululta. There, as night fell, Arha removed his clothes and stood in the damp cold wind that swept across the plateau with the setting sun. Across the valley, several miles away, Arha saw the light of his friend's fire, which shone like a star in the blackness.

The wind turned colder and seemed to pass through his flesh and chill the marrow in his bones. The rock on which he stood felt like ice.

The Fire on the Mountain

Each hour the cold numbed him more, until he thought he would never be warm again, but he kept his eyes upon the twinkling light across the valley, and remembered that his old friend sat there tending a fire for him. Sometimes wisps of fog blotted out the light, and then he strained to see until the fog passed. He sneezed and coughed and shivered, and began to feel ill. Yet all night through he stood there, and only when the dawn came did he put on his clothes and go down the mountain back to Addis Ababa.

Haptom was very surprised to see Arha, and he questioned his servants thoroughly.

"Did he stay all night without food or drink or blankets or clothing?"

"Yes," his servants said. "He did all of these things."

"Well, you are a strong fellow," Hamptom said to Arha. "How did you manage to do it?"

"I simply watched the light of a fire on a distant hill," Arha said.

"What! You watched a fire? Then you lose the bet, and you are still my servant, and you own no land!"

"But this fire was not close enough to warm me, it was far across the valley!"

"I won't give you the land," Haptom said.

"You didn't fulfill the conditions. It was only the fire that saved you."

Arha was very sad. He went again to his old friend of the Guragé tribe and told him what had happened.

"Take the matter to the judge," the old man advised him.

Arha went to the judge and complained, and the judge sent for Haptom. When Haptom told his story, and the servants said once more that Arha had watched a distant fire across the valley, the judge said:

"No, you have lost, for Haptom Hasei's condition was that you must be without fire."

Once more Arha went to his old friend with the sad news that he was doomed to the life of a servant, as though he had not gone through the ordeal on the mountaintop.

"Don't give up hope," the old man said. "More wisdom grows wild in the hills than in any city judge."

He got up from where he sat and went to find a man named Hailu, in whose house he had been a servant when he was young. He explained to the good man about the bet between Haptom and Arha, and asked if something couldn't be done.

"Don't worry about it," Hailu said after

The Fire on the Mountain

thinking for a while. "I will take care of it for you."

Some days later Hailu sent invitations to many people in the city to come to a feast at his house. Haptom was among them, and so was the judge who had ruled Arha had lost the bet.

When the day of the feast arrived, the guests came riding on mules with fine trappings, their servants strung out behind them on foot. Haptom came with twenty servants, one of whom held a silk umbrella over his head to shade him from the sun, and four drummers played music that signified the great Haptom was here.

The guests sat on soft rugs laid out for them and talked. From the kitchen came the odors of wonderful things to eat: roast goat, roast corn and durra, pancakes called injera, and many tantalizing sauces. The smell of the food only accentuated the hunger of the guests. Time passed. The food should have been served, but they didn't see it, only smelled vapors that drifted from the kitchen. The evening came, and still no food was served. The guests began to whisper among themselves. It was very curious that the honorable Hailu had not had the food brought out. Still the smells came from the kitchen. At last one of the guests spoke out for all the others:

"Hailu, why do you do this to us? Why do you invite us to a feast and then serve us nothing?"

"Why, can't you smell the food?" Hailu asked with surprise.

"Indeed we can, but smelling is not eating, there is not nourishment in it!"

"And is there warmth in a fire so distant that it can hardly be seen?" Hailu asked. "If Arha was warmed by the fire he watched while standing on Mount Sululta, then you have been fed by the smells coming from my kitchen."

The people agreed with him; the judge now saw his mistake, and Haptom was shamed. He thanked Hailu for his advice, and announced that Arha was then and there the owner of the land, the house, and the cattle.

Then Hailu ordered the food brought in, and the feast began.

JANOT COOKS FOR THE EMPEROR

In the old days, when the Emperor was alive, there was a cook in the palace at Sans Souci by the name of Janot. One day while the Emperor was eating dinner with his wife, he said: "Today I went to the top of the mountain to supervise the building of the fortress. It was very cold up there."

Janot, the cook, said, "Emperor, it's really not cold up there at all."

The Emperor replied, "Who is this who contradicts the Emperor?"

Janot said, "It is I, Janot, the cook."

The Emperor said, "Janot, when I say it is cold, it is cold."

Janot said, "Emperor, it's not so cold."

The Emperor said, "If a man had to stay up there all night without clothes or heat of any kind, he would die."

"Oh, no," Janot said, "it's really not so cold."

The Emperor became annoyed.

"Who are you to argue with the Emperor?" he

"Janot Cooks for the Emperor" from THE PIECE OF FIRE, copyright 1964 by Harold Courlander. Reprinted by permission of Harcourt Brace Jovanovich, Inc.

said. "Tonight you will go up there on top of the mountain and stay there without clothing or fire until dawn. If you are still alive when the sun comes up, I will give you a hundred acres of ground for your own. But if you are dead, as you certainly will be, we shall write on your tomb, 'Here lies the fool that argues with the Emperor.'"

In the evening two soldiers took Janot to the top of the mountain. They went to the highest tower of the fortress. Janot took off his clothes. "See," he said. "It's not very cold."

But when the sun went down, the wind began to blow, and the damp mists gathered around the mountain peak. Janot began to shiver. The soldiers laughed. "Why are you shaking that way?" they asked.

"Oh, I do that to keep warm," Janot said.

In a little while his jaw was trembling and his teeth were rattling together.

"Why are your teeth doing that?" the soldiers said.

"Oh, I do that because it is so quiet up here," Janot replied.

Soon tears were running from Janot's eyes because of the cold wind.

"What is happening?" the soldiers asked.

Janot Cooks for the Emperor 57

"Oh, I am just thinking of my dear dead mother," Janot answered.

Janot began slapping his sides with his hands to warm himself.

"What are you doing now?" the soldiers said.

"Oh, this is what my fighting cock does when he is feeling good," Janot said.

As the hours went by, Janot felt worse and worse. When the sun came up at last, he was lying unconscious on his back. The soldiers put him on a horse and took him back to the palace.

"Ah," the Emperor said, "here is my stupid cook, dead as I expected."

"No, not dead," Janot said, opening his eyes. "Just resting."

"It looks to me, in any case, as though you found it was mighty cold up there," the Emperor said.

"No," Janot said. "On the contrary, it was rather warm."

The Emperor became angry.

"What did he do up there on the mountain?" he asked the soldiers.

"He shivered, he shook, he clacked his teeth, he slapped his sides, and he cried," they said.

"What else?" the Emperor demanded.

"Nothing else," Janot said. "Except that

sometimes I looked down at the lights in the palace."

"Oh, now it is clear!" the Emperor said. "You were kept warm by the oil lamps and the charcoal fires in the palace! You didn't stay with the conditions! Janot, you have lost the bet."

"Emperor," Janot said, "the lights I saw were many miles away. How could they keep me warm?"

"It is finished," the Emperor said. "You didn't live by the rules. Therefore, you don't get the hundred acres of land."

That evening when it was time for dinner, the Emperor and his wife went to the palace dining room and sat at the table. When they had sat for a while, the Emperor called one of the servants and asked, "Where is the dinner?"

"Janot says it isn't cooked yet," the servant answered.

The Emperor and his wife waited. An hour went by. The Emperor called out again, "Where is the food?"

"Janot says it is still cooking," the servant said.

More time went by. The Emperor was getting more and more angry. At last he got up and went out to the kitchen. Janot was sitting patiently, waiting for the meal to be cooked. But the pot

Janot Cooks for the Emperor

with the food in it was at one end of the room, while the charcoal fire was at the other. The food was raw and cold.

"What kind of stupidity is this!" the Emperor shouted. "How will the food ever get cooked if it isn't on the fire?"

"Be a little patient, Emperor," Janot said. "After all, the pot and the fire are only a little distance apart."

"And do you think the food will ever get cooked this way?" the Emperor shouted.

"Emperor," Janot said, "if I could be warmed by the palace lights while I was standing up there on top of the mountain, surely this fire will be able to cook the dinner!"

The Emperor was silent. Then he laughed.

"Put the pot on the fire, Janot," he said. "The hundred acres of ground are yours."

BEAUTY AND THE BEAST

ONCE UPON A TIME, in a far-off country, there lived a merchant who was enormously rich. As he had six sons and six daughters, however, who were accustomed to having everything they fancied, he did not find he had a penny too much. But misfortunes befell them. One day their house caught fire and speedily burned to the ground, with all the splendid furniture, books, pictures, gold, silver and precious goods it contained. The father suddenly lost every ship he had upon the sea, either by dint of pirates, shipwreck or fire. Then he heard that his clerks in distant countries, whom he had trusted entirely, had proved unfaithful. And at last from great wealth he fell into the direst poverty.

All that he had left was a little house in a desolate place at least a hundred leagues from the town. The daughters at first hoped their friends, who had been so numerous while they were rich, would insist on their staying in their houses, but they soon found they were left alone. Their former friends even attributed their misfortunes to their own extrava-

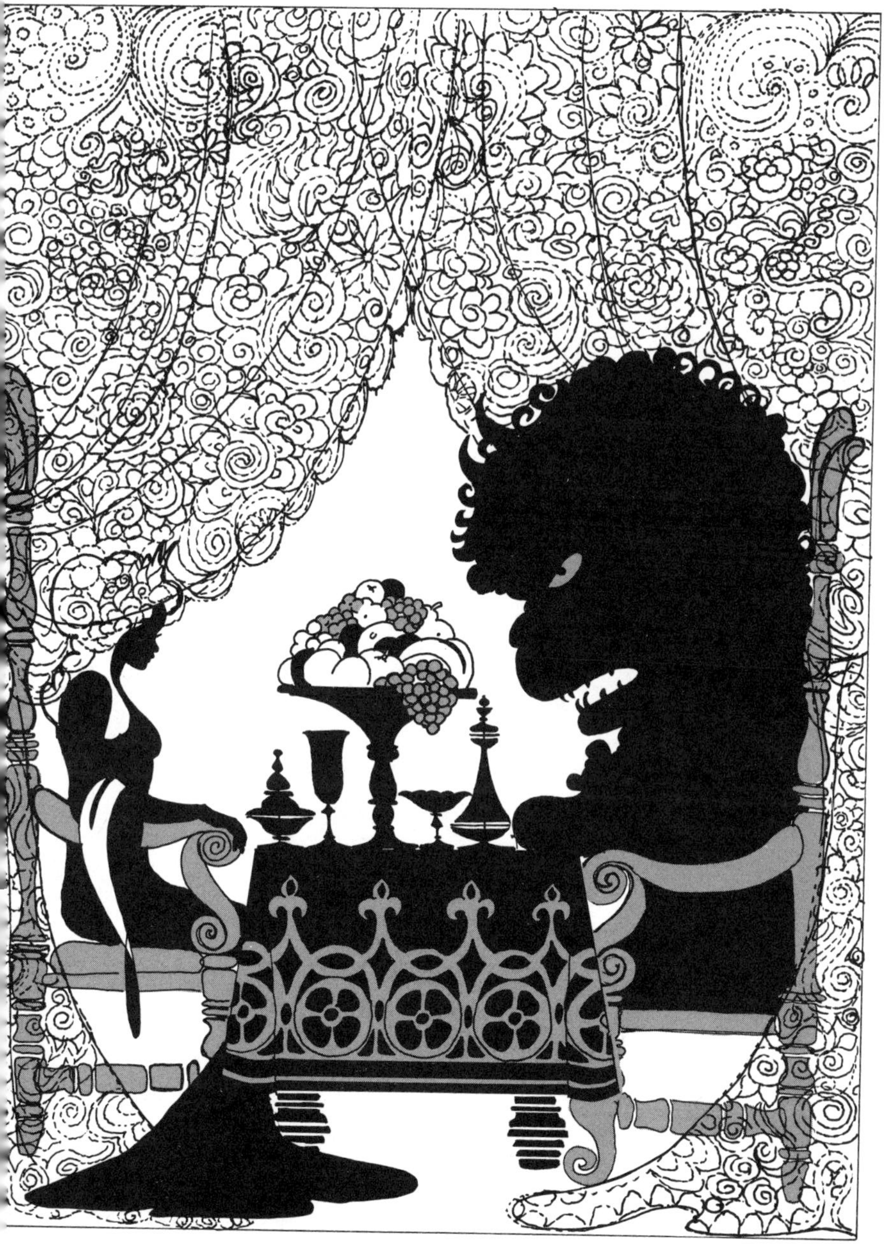

gance and showed no intention of offering them any help.

So nothing was left for them but to take their departure to the cottage, which stood in the midst of a dark forest. As they were too poor to have any servants, the girls had to work hard, and the sons, for their part, cultivated the fields to earn their living. Roughly clothed, and living in the simplest way, the girls regretted unceasingly the luxuries and amusements of their former life. Only the youngest daughter tried to be brave and cheerful.

She had been as sad as anyone when misfortune first overtook her father, but soon recovering her natural gaiety, she set to work to make the best of things, to amuse her father and brothers as well as she could, and to persuade her sisters to join her in dancing and singing. But they would do nothing of the sort, and because she was not as doleful as themselves, they declared this miserable life was all she was fit for. But she was really far prettier and cleverer than they were. Indeed, she was so lovely she was always called Beauty.

After two years, their father received news that one of his ships, which he had believed lost, had come safely into port with a rich cargo. All the sons and daughters at once thought that their poverty was at an end and wanted to set out directly for the town; but their father, who was more prudent, begged them to wait a little, and though it was harvest time, and he could ill be spared, determined to go himself to make inquiries.

Only the youngest daughter had any doubt but that they would soon again be as rich as they were before. They all loaded their father with commissions for jewels and dresses which it would have taken a fortune to buy; only Beauty did not ask for anything. Her father, noticing her silence, said:

'And what shall I bring for you, Beauty?'

'The only thing I wish for is to see you come home safely,' she answered.

But this reply vexed her sisters, who fancied she was blaming them for having asked for such costly things. Her father, however, was pleased, but as he thought she certainly ought to like pretty presents, he told her to choose something.

'Well, dear Father,' she said, 'as you insist upon it, I beg that you will bring me a rose. I have not seen one since we came here, and I love them so much.'

The merchant set out, only to find that his former companions, believing him to be dead, had divided his cargo between them. After six months of trouble and expense he found himself as poor as when he

Beauty and the Beast

started on his journey. To make matters worse, he was obliged to return in the most terrible weather. By the time he was within a few leagues of his home he was almost exhausted with cold and fatigue. Though he knew it would take some hours to get through the forest, he resolved to go on. But night overtook him, and the deep snow and bitter frost made it impossible for his horse to carry him any farther.

The only shelter he could get was the hollow trunk of a great tree, and there he crouched all the night, which seemed to him the longest he had ever known. The howling of the wolves kept him awake, and when at last day broke the falling snow had covered up every path, and he did not know which way to turn.

At length he made out some sort of path, but it was so rough and slippery that he fell down more than once. Presently it led him into an avenue of trees which ended in a splendid castle. It seemed to the merchant very strange that no snow had fallen in the avenue of orange trees, covered with flowers and fruit. When he reached the first court of the castle he saw before him a flight of agate steps. He went up them and passed through several splendidly furnished rooms.

The pleasant warmth of the air revived him, and he felt very hungry; but there seemed to be nobody in all this vast and splendid palace. Deep silence reigned everywhere, and at last, tired of roaming through empty rooms and galleries, he stopped in a room smaller than the rest, where a clear fire was burning and a couch was drawn up cosily before it. Thinking this must be prepared for someone who was expected, he sat down to wait till he should come and very soon fell into a sweet sleep.

When his extreme hunger wakened him after several hours, he was still alone; but a little table, with a good dinner on it, had been drawn up close to him. He lost no time in beginning his meal, hoping he might soon thank his considerate host, whoever it might be. But no one appeared, and even after another long sleep, from which he awoke completely refreshed, there was no sign of anybody, though a fresh meal of dainty cakes and fruit was prepared upon the little table at his elbow.

Being naturally timid, the silence began to terrify him, and he resolved to search once more through all the rooms; but it was of no use, there was no sign of life in the palace! Then he went down into the garden, and though it was winter everywhere else, here the sun shone, the birds sang, the flowers

Beauty and the Beast

bloomed, and the air was soft and sweet. The merchant, in ecstasies with all he saw and heard, said to himself:

'All this must be meant for me. I will go this minute and bring my children to share all these delights.'

In spite of being so cold and weary when he reached the castle, he had taken his horse to the stable and fed it. Now he thought he would saddle it for his homeward journey, and he turned down the path which led to the stable. This path had a hedge of roses on each side of it, and the merchant thought he had never seen such exquisite flowers. They reminded him of his promise to Beauty, and he stopped and had just gathered one to take to her when he was startled by a strange noise behind him. Turning round, he saw a frightful Beast, which seemed to be very angry and said in a terrible voice:

'Who told you you might gather my roses? Was it not enough that I sheltered you in my palace and was kind to you? This is the way you show your gratitude, by stealing my flowers! But your insolence shall not go unpunished.'

The merchant, terrified by these furious words, dropped the fatal rose and, throwing himself on his knees, cried, 'Pardon me, noble sir. I am truly grateful for your hospitality, which was so magnificent I could not imagine you would be offended by my taking such a little thing as a rose.'

But the Beast's anger was not lessened by his speech.

'You are very ready with excuses and flattery,' he cried. 'But that will not save you from the death you deserve.'

Alas, thought the merchant, if my daughter Beauty could only know into what danger her rose has brought me! And in despair he began to tell the Beast all his misfortunes and the reason of his journey, not forgetting to mention Beauty's request.

'A king's ransom would hardly have procured all that my other daughters asked for,' he said. 'But I thought I might at least take Beauty her rose. I beg you to forgive me, for you see I meant no harm.'

The Beast said, in a less furious tone, 'I will forgive you on one condition—that you will give me one of your daughters.'

'Ah,' cried the merchant, 'if I were cruel enough to buy my own life at the expense of one of my children's, what excuse could I invent to bring her here?'

'None,' answered the Beast. 'If she comes at all she must come willingly. On no other condition will I have her. See if any one of them is courageous

Beauty and the Beast

enough, and loves you enough, to come and save your life. You seem to be an honest man so I will trust you to go home. I give you a month to see if any of your daughters will come back with you and stay here, to let you go free. If none of them is willing, you must come alone, after bidding them good-bye forever, for then you will belong to me. And do not imagine that you can hide from me, for if you fail to keep your word I will come and fetch you!' added the Beast grimly.

The merchant accepted this proposal. He promised to return at the time appointed, and then, anxious to escape from the presence of the Beast, he asked permission to set off at once. But the Beast answered that he could not go until the next day.

'Then you will find a horse ready for you,' he said. 'Now go and eat your supper and await my orders.'

The poor merchant, more dead than alive, went back to his room, where the most delicious supper was already served on the little table drawn up before a blazing fire. But he was too terrified to eat and only tasted a few of the dishes, for fear the Beast should be angry if he did not obey his orders. When he had finished, the Beast warned him to remember their agreement and to prepare his daughter exactly for what she had to expect.

'Do not get up tomorrow,' he added, 'until you see the sun and hear a golden bell ring. Then you will find your breakfast waiting for you, and the horse you are to ride will be ready in the courtyard. He will also bring you back again when you come with your daughter a month hence. Farewell. Take a rose to Beauty, and remember your promise!'

The merchant lay down until the sun rose. Then, after breakfast, he went to gather Beauty's rose and mounted his horse, which carried him off so swiftly that in an instant he had lost sight of the palace. He was still wrapped in gloomy thoughts when it stopped before the door of his cottage.

His sons and daughters, who had been uneasy at his long absence, rushed to meet him, eager to know the result of his journey which, seeing him mounted upon a splendid horse and wrapped in a rich mantle, they supposed to be favorable. But he hid the truth from them at first, only saying sadly to Beauty as he gave her the rose:

'Here is what you asked me to bring you. Little you know what it has cost.'

Presently he told them his adventures from beginning to end, and then they were all very unhappy. The girls lamented loudly over their lost hopes, and the sons declared their father should not return to the terrible castle. But he reminded them he had promised to go back. Then the girls were very angry with Beauty and said it was all her fault. If she had asked for something sensible this would never have happened.

Poor Beauty, much distressed, said to them, 'I have indeed caused this misfortune, but who could have guessed that to ask for a rose in the middle of summer would cause so much misery? But as I did the mischief it is only just that I should suffer for it. I will therefore go back with my father to keep his promise.'

At first nobody would hear of it. Her father and brothers, who loved her dearly, declared nothing should make them let her go. But Beauty was firm. As the time drew near she divided her little possessions between her sisters, and said good-bye to everything she loved. When the fatal day came she encouraged and cheered her father as they mounted together the horse which had brought him back. It seemed to fly rather than gallop, but so smoothly that Beauty was not frightened. Indeed, she would have enjoyed the journey if she had not feared what might happen at the end of it. Her father still tried to persuade her to go back, but in vain.

While they were talking the night fell. Then, to their great surprise, wonderful colored lights began to shine in all directions, and splendid fireworks blazed out before them; all the forest was illuminated. They even felt pleasantly warm, though it had been bitterly cold before. They reached the avenue of orange trees and saw that the palace was brilliantly lighted from roof to ground, and music sounded softly from the courtyard.

'The Beast must be very hungry,' said Beauty, trying to laugh, 'if he makes all this rejoicing over the arrival of his prey.' But, in spite of her anxiety, she admired all the wonderful things she saw.

When they had dismounted, her father led her to the little room. Here they found a splendid fire burning, and the table daintily spread with a delicious supper.

Beauty, who was less frightened now that she had passed through so many rooms and seen nothing of the Beast, was quite willing to begin, for her long ride had made her very hungry. But they had hardly finished their meal when the noise of the Beast's footsteps was heard approaching, and Beauty clung to her father in terror, which became all the greater when she saw how frightened he was. But when the Beast really appeared, though she trembled at the sight of him, she made a great effort to hide her horror, and saluted him respectfully.

This evidently pleased the Beast. After looking at her he said, in a tone that might have struck

Beauty and the Beast

terror into the boldest heart, though he did not seem to be angry:

'Good evening, old man. Good evening, Beauty.'

The merchant was too terrified to reply, but Beauty answered sweetly, 'Good evening, Beast.'

'Have you come willingly?' asked the Beast. 'Will you be content to stay here when your father goes away?'

Beauty answered bravely that she was quite prepared to stay.

'I am pleased with you,' said the Beast. 'As you have come of your own accord, you may remain. As for you, old man,' he added, turning to the merchant, 'at sunrise tomorrow take your departure. When the bell rings, get up quickly and eat your breakfast, and you will find the same horse waiting to take you home.'

Then turning to Beauty, he said, 'Take your father into the next room, and help him choose gifts for your brothers and sisters. You will find two traveling trunks there; fill them as full as you can. It is only just that you should send them something very precious as a remembrance.'

Then he went away, after saying, 'Good-bye, Beauty; good-bye, old man.' Beauty was beginning to think with great dismay of her father's departure, but they went into the next room, which had shelves and cupboards all round it. They were greatly surprised at the riches it contained. There were splendid dresses fit for a queen, with all the ornaments to be worn with them, and when Beauty opened the cupboards she was dazzled by the gorgeous jewels lying in heaps upon every shelf. After choosing a vast quantity, which she divided between her sisters—for she had made a heap of the wonderful dresses for each of them—she opened the last chest, which was full of gold.

'I think, Father,' she said, 'that, as the gold will be more useful to you, we had better take out the other things again, and fill the trunks with it.'

So they did this, but the more they put in, the more room there seemed to be, and at last they put back all the jewels and dresses they had taken out, and Beauty even added as many more of the jewels as she could carry at once. Even then the trunks were not too full, but they were so heavy an elephant could not have carried them!

'The Beast was mocking us!' cried the merchant. 'He pretended to give us all these things, knowing that I could not carry them away.'

'Let us wait and see,' answered Beauty. 'I cannot believe he meant to deceive us. All we can do is to fasten them up and have them ready.'

So they did this and returned to the little room

where they found breakfast ready. The merchant ate his with a good appetite, as the Beast's generosity made him believe he might perhaps venture to come back soon and see Beauty. But she felt sure her father was leaving her forever, so she was very sad when the bell rang sharply.

They went down into the courtyard, where two horses were waiting, one loaded with the two trunks, the other for him to ride. They were pawing the ground in their impatience to start, and the merchant bade Beauty a hasty farewell. As soon as he was mounted he went off at such a pace she lost sight of him in an instant. Then Beauty began to cry and wandered sadly back to her own room. But she soon found she was very sleepy, and as she had nothing better to do she lay down and instantly fell asleep. And then she dreamed she was walking by a brook bordered with trees, and lamenting her sad fate, when a young prince, handsomer than anyone she had ever seen, and with a voice that went straight to her heart, came and said to her:

'Ah, Beauty, you are not so unfortunate as you suppose. Here you will be rewarded for all you have suffered elsewhere. Your every wish shall be gratified. Only try to find me out, no matter how I may be disguised, for I love you dearly, and in making me happy you will find your own happiness. Be as true-hearted as you are beautiful, and we shall have nothing left to wish for.'

'What can I do, Prince, to make you happy?' said Beauty.

'Only be grateful,' he answered, 'and do not trust too much to your eyes. Above all, do not desert me until you have saved me from my cruel misery.'

After this she thought she found herself in a room with a stately and beautiful lady, who said to her, 'Dear Beauty, try not to regret all you have left behind you; you are destined for a better fate. Only do not let yourself be deceived by appearances.'

Beauty found her dreams so interesting that she was in no hurry to awake, but presently the clock roused her by calling her name softly twelve times. Then she rose and found her dressing-table set out with everything she could possibly want, and when her toilet was finished, she found dinner waiting in the room next to hers. But dinner does not take very long when one is alone, and very soon she sat down cosily in the corner of a sofa, and began to think about the charming prince she had seen in her dream.

'He said I could make him happy,' said Beauty to herself. 'It seems, then, that this horrible Beast keeps him a prisoner. How can I set him free? I wonder why they both told me not to trust to appearances? But, after all, it was only a dream, so why should I trouble myself about it? I had better find something to do to amuse myself.'

So she began to explore some of the many rooms of the palace. The first she entered was lined with mirrors. Beauty saw herself reflected on every side and thought she had never seen such a charming room. Then a bracelet which was hanging from a chandelier caught her eye, and on taking it down she was greatly surprised to find that it held a portrait of her unknown admirer, just as she had seen him in her dream. With great delight she slipped the bracelet on her arm and went on into a gallery of pictures, where she soon found a portrait of the same handsome prince, as large as life, and so well painted that as she studied it he seemed to smile kindly at her.

Tearing herself away from the portrait at last, she passed into a room which contained every musical instrument under the sun, and here she amused herself for a long while in trying them and singing. The next room was a library, and she saw everything she had ever wanted to read as well as everything she had read. By this time it was growing dusk, and wax candles in diamond and ruby candlesticks lit themselves in every room.

Beauty found her supper served just at the time

she preferred to have it, but she did not see anyone or hear a sound, and though her father had warned her she would be alone, she began to find it rather dull.

Presently she heard the Beast coming and wondered tremblingly if he meant to eat her now. However, he did not seem at all ferocious, and only said gruffly:

'Good evening, Beauty.'

She answered cheerfully and managed to conceal her terror. The Beast asked how she had been amusing herself, and she told him all the rooms she had seen. Then he asked if she thought she could be happy in his palace; and Beauty answered that everything was so beautiful she would be very hard to please if she could not be happy. After about an hour's talk Beauty began to think the Beast was not nearly so terrible as she had supposed at first. Then he rose to leave her, and said in his gruff voice:

'Do you love me, Beauty? Will you marry me?'

'Oh, what shall I say?' cried Beauty, for she was afraid to make the Beast angry by refusing.

'Say yes or no without fear,' he replied.

'Oh, no, Beast,' said Beauty hastily.

'Since you will not, good night, Beauty,' he said.

And she answered, 'Good night, Beast,' very glad to find her refusal had not provoked him. After he was gone she was very soon in bed and dreaming of her unknown prince.

She thought he came and said, 'Ah, Beauty! Why are you so unkind to me? I fear I am fated to be unhappy for many a long day still.'

Then her dreams changed, but the charming prince figured in them all. When morning came her first thought was to look at the portrait and see if it was really like him, and she found it certainly was.

She decided to amuse herself in the garden, for the sun shone, and all the fountains were playing. She was astonished to find that every place was familiar to her, and presently she came to the very brook and the myrtle trees where she had first met the prince in her dream. That made her think more than ever he must be kept a prisoner by the Beast.

When she was tired she went back to the palace and found a new room full of materials for every kind of work—ribbons to make into bows and silks to work into flowers. There was an aviary full of rare birds, which were so tame they flew to Beauty as soon as they saw her and perched upon her shoulders and her head.

'Pretty little creatures,' she said, 'how I wish your cage was nearer my room that I might often hear you sing!' So saying she opened a door and found to her delight that it led into her own room, though she had thought it was on the other side of the palace.

There were more birds in a room farther on, parrots and cockatoos that could talk, and they greeted Beauty by name. Indeed, she found them so entertaining that she took one or two back to her room, and they talked to her while she was at supper. The Beast paid her his usual visit and asked the same questions as before, and then with a gruff good night he took his departure, and Beauty went to bed to dream of her mysterious prince.

The days passed swiftly in different amusements, and after a while Beauty found another strange thing in the palace, which often pleased her when she was tired of being alone. There was one room which she had not noticed particularly; it was empty, except that under each of the windows stood a very comfortable chair. The first time she had looked out of the window it seemed a black curtain prevented her from seeing anything outside. But the second time she went into the room, happening to be tired, she sat down in one of the chairs, when instantly the curtain was rolled aside, and a most amusing pantomime was acted before her. There were dances and colored lights, music and pretty dresses, and it was all so gay that Beauty was in ecstasies. After that she tried the other seven windows in turn, and there was some new and surprising entertainment to be seen from each of them so Beauty never could feel lonely any more. Every evening after supper the Beast came to see her, and always before saying good night asked her in his terrible voice:

'Beauty, will you marry me?'

And it seemed to Beauty, now she understood him better, that when she said, 'No, Beast,' he went away quite sad. Her happy dreams of the handsome young prince soon made her forget the poor Beast, and the only thing that disturbed her was being told to distrust appearances, to let her heart guide her, and not her eyes. Consider as she would, she could not understand.

So everything went on for a long time, until at last, happy as she was, Beauty began to long for the sight of her father and her brothers and sisters. One night, seeing her look very sad, the Beast asked her what was the matter. Beauty had quite ceased to be afraid of him. Now she knew he was really gentle in spite of his ferocious looks and his dreadful voice. So she answered that she wished to see her home once more. Upon hearing this the Beast seemed sadly distressed, and cried miserably:

'Ah, Beauty, have you the heart to desert an unhappy Beast like this? What more do you want to make you happy? Is it because you hate me that you want to escape?'

'No, dear Beast,' answered Beauty softly, 'I do not hate you, and I should be very sorry never to see you any more, but I long to see my father again. Only let me go for two months, and I promise to come back to you and stay for the rest of my life.'

The Beast, who had been sighing dolefully while she spoke, now replied, 'I cannot refuse you anything you ask, even though it should cost me my life. Take the four boxes you will find in the room next to your own and fill them with everything you wish to take with you. But remember your promise and come back when the two months are over, for if you do not come in good time you will find your faithful Beast dead. You will not need any chariot to bring you back. Only say good-bye to all your brothers and sisters the night before you come away and, when you have gone to bed, turn this ring round upon your finger, and say firmly, "I wish to go back to my palace and see my Beast again." Good night, Beauty. Fear nothing, sleep peacefully, and before long you shall see your father once more.'

As soon as Beauty was alone she hastened to fill the boxes with all the rare and precious things she saw about her, and only when she was tired of

Beauty and the Beast

heaping things into them did they seem to be full. Then she went to bed, but could hardly sleep for joy. When at last she began to dream of her beloved prince she was grieved to see him stretched upon a grassy bank, sad and weary, and hardly like himself.

'What is the matter?' she cried.

But he looked at her reproachfully, and said, 'How can you ask me, cruel one? Are you not leaving me to my death perhaps?'

'Ah, don't be so sorrowful!' cried Beauty. 'I am only going to assure my father that I am safe and happy. I have promised the Beast faithfully I will come back, and he would die of grief if I did not keep my word!'

'What would that matter to you?' asked the prince. 'Surely you would not care?'

'Indeed I should be ungrateful if I did not care for such a kind Beast,' cried Beauty indignantly. 'I would die to save him from pain. I assure you it is not his fault he is so ugly.'

Just then a strange sound woke her—someone was speaking not very far away; and opening her eyes she found herself in a room she had never seen before, which was certainly not as splendid as those she had seen in the Beast's palace. Where could she be? She rose and dressed hastily and then saw that the boxes she had packed the night before were all in the room. Suddenly she heard her father's voice and rushed out to greet him joyfully. Her brothers and sisters were astonished at her appearance, for they had never expected to see her again. Beauty asked her father what he thought her strange dreams meant and why the prince constantly begged her not to trust to appearances. After much consideration he answered:

'You tell me yourself that the Beast, frightful as he is, loves you dearly and deserves your love and gratitude for his gentleness and kindness. I think the prince must mean you to understand you ought to reward him by doing as he wishes, in spite of his ugliness.'

Beauty could not help seeing that this seemed probable; still, when she thought of her dear prince who was so handsome, she did not feel at all inclined to marry the Beast. At any rate, for two months she need not decide but could enjoy herself with her sisters. Though they were rich now, and lived in a town again and had plenty of acquaintances, Beauty found that nothing amused her very much. She often thought of the palace, where she was so happy, especially as at home she never once dreamed of her dear prince, and she felt quite sad without him.

Then her sisters seemed quite used to being without her, and even found her rather in the way, so she would not have been sorry when the two months were over but for her father and brothers. She had not the courage to say good-bye to them. Every day when she rose she meant to say it at night, and when night came she put it off again, until at last she had a dismal dream which helped her to make up her mind.

She thought she was wandering in a lonely path in the palace gardens, when she heard groans. Running quickly to see what could be the matter, she found the Beast stretched out upon his side, apparently dying. He reproached her faintly with being the cause of his distress, and at the same moment a stately lady appeared, and said very gravely:

'Ah, Beauty, see what happens when people do not keep their promises! If you had delayed one day more, you would have found him dead.'

Beauty was so terrified by this dream that the very next evening she said good-bye to her father and her brothers and sisters, and as soon as she was in bed she turned her ring round upon her finger, and said firmly:

'I wish to go back to my palace and see my Beast again.'

Then she fell asleep instantly, and only woke up to hear the clock saying, 'Beauty, Beauty,' twelve times in its musical voice, which told her she was really in the palace once more. Everything was just as before, and her birds were so glad to see her, but Beauty thought she had never known such a long day. She was so anxious to see the Beast again that she felt as if suppertime would never come.

But when it came no Beast appeared. After listening and waiting for a long time, she ran down into the garden to search for him. Up and down the paths and avenues ran poor Beauty, calling him. No one answered, and not a trace of him could she find. At last, she saw that she was standing opposite the shady path she had seen in her dream. She rushed down it and, sure enough, there was the cave, and in it lay the Beast—asleep, so Beauty thought. Quite glad to have found him, she ran up and stroked his head, but to her horror he did not move or open his eyes.

'Oh, he is dead, and it is all my fault!' cried Beauty, crying bitterly.

But then, looking at him again, she fancied he still breathed. Hastily fetching some water from the nearest fountain, she sprinkled it over his face, and to her great delight he began to revive.

'Oh, Beast, how you frightened me!' she cried. 'I never knew how much I loved you until just now, when I feared I was too late to save your life.'

'Can you really love such an ugly creature as I am?' asked the Beast faintly. 'Ah, Beauty, you came only just in time. I was dying because I thought you had forgotten your promise. But go back now and rest, I shall see you again by-and-by.'

Beauty, who had half expected he would be angry with her, was reassured by his gentle voice and went back to the palace, where supper was awaiting her. And afterward the Beast came in as usual and talked about the time she had spent with her father, asking if she had enjoyed herself and if they had all been glad to see her.

Beauty quite enjoyed telling him all that had happened to her. When at last the time came for him to go, he asked, as he had so often asked before:

'Beauty, will you marry me?'

She answered softly, 'Yes, dear Beast.'

As she spoke a blaze of light sprang up before the windows of the palace; fireworks crackled and guns banged, and across the avenue of orange trees, in letters all made of fireflies, was written: *Long live the prince and his bride.*

Turning to ask the Beast what it could all mean,

Beauty found he had disappeared, and in his place stood her long-loved prince! At the same moment the wheels of a chariot were heard upon the terrace, and two ladies entered the room. One of them Beauty recognized as the stately lady she had seen in her dreams; the other was so queenly that Beauty hardly knew which to greet first. But the one she already knew said to her companion:

'Well, Queen, this is Beauty, who has had the courage to rescue your son from the terrible enchantment. They love each other, and only your consent to their marriage is wanting to make them perfectly happy.'

'I consent with all my heart,' cried the queen. 'How can I ever thank you enough, charming girl, for having restored my dear son to his natural form?' And then she tenderly embraced Beauty and the prince, who had meanwhile been greeting the fairy and receiving her congratulations.

'Now,' said the fairy to Beauty, 'I suppose you would like me to send for all your brothers and sisters to dance at your wedding?'

And so she did, and the marriage was celebrated the very next day with the utmost splendor, and Beauty and the prince lived happily ever after.

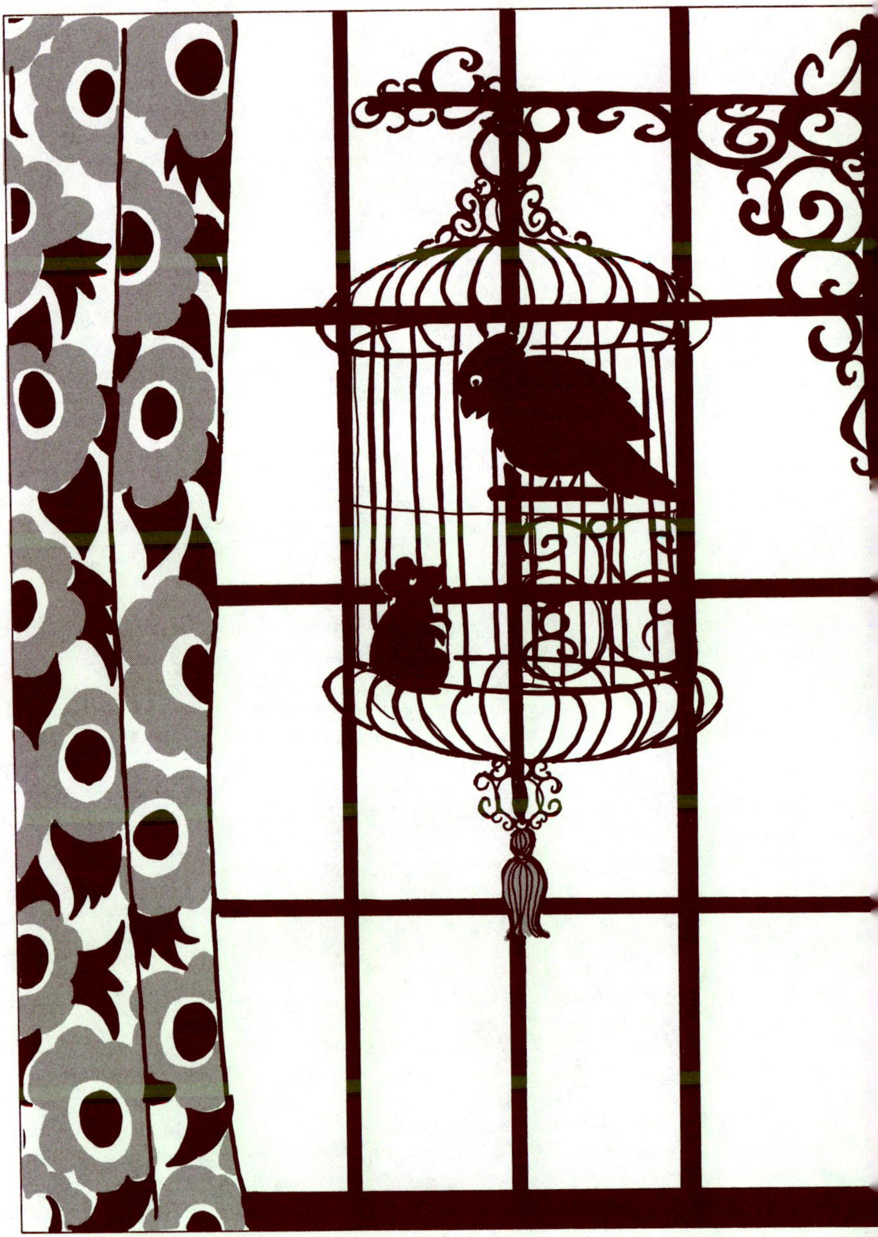

THE MOUSEWIFE

Wherever there is an old house with wooden floors and beams and rafters and wooden stairs and wainscots and skirting boards and larders, there are mice. They creep out on the carpets for crumbs, they whisk in and out of their holes, they run in the wainscot and between the ceiling and the floors. There are no signposts because they know the way, and no milestones because no one is there to see how they run.

In the old nursery rhyme, when the cat went to see the queen, he caught a little mouse under her chair; that was long long ago and that queen was different from our queen, but the mouse was the same.

Mice have always been the same. There are no fashions in mice, they do not change. If a mouse could have a portrait painted of his great-great-grandfather, and *his* great-grandfather, it would be the portrait of a mouse today.

But once there was a little mousewife who was different from the rest.

She looked the same; she had the same ears and prick nose and whiskers and dewdrop eyes; the same little bones and grey fur; the same skinny paws and long skinny tail.

She did all the things a mousewife does: she made a nest for the mouse babies she hoped to have one day; she collected crumbs of food for her husband and herself; once she bit the tops off a whole bowl of crocuses; and she played with the other mice at midnight on the attic floor.

"What more do you want?" asked her husband.

She did not know what it was she wanted, but she wanted more.

The house where these mice lived belonged to a spinster lady called Miss Barbara Wilkinson. The mice thought the house was the whole world. The garden and the wood that lay round it were as far away to them as the stars are to you, but the mousewife used sometimes to creep up on the window sill and press her whiskers close against the pane.

In spring she saw snowdrops and appleblossom in the garden and bluebells in the wood; in summer there were roses; in autumn all the trees changed colour; and in winter they were bare until the snow came and they were white with snow.

The mousewife saw all these through the windowpane, but she did not know what they were.

She was a house mouse, not a garden mouse or a field mouse; she could not go outside.

"I think about cheese," said her husband. "Why don't you think about cheese?"

Then, at Christmas, he had an attack of indigestion through eating rich crumbs of Christmas cake. "There were currants in those crumbs," said the mousewife. "They have upset you. You must go to bed and be kept warm." She decided to move the mousehole to a space behind the fender where it was warm. She lined the new hole with tufts of carpet wool and put her husband to bed wrapped in a pattern of grey flannel that Miss Wilkinson's lazy maid, Flora, had left in the dustpan. "But I am grateful to Flora," said the mousewife's husband as he settled himself comfortably in bed.

Now the mousewife had to find all the food for the family in addition to keeping the hole swept and clean.

She had no time for thinking.

While she was busy, a boy brought a dove to Miss Wilkinson. He had caught it in the wood. It was a pretty thing, a turtledove. Miss Wilkinson put it in a cage on the ledge of her sitting room window.

The cage was an elegant one; it had gilt bars and a door that opened if its catch were pressed down; there were small gilt trays for water and peas. Miss Wilkinson hung up a lump of sugar and a piece of fat. "There, you have everything you want," said Miss Barbara Wilkinson.

For a day or two the dove pecked at the bars and opened and shut its wings. Sometimes it called "Roo coo, roo coo"; then it was silent.

"Why won't it eat?" asked Miss Barbara Wilkinson. "Those are the very best peas."

A mouse family seldom has enough to eat. It is difficult to come by crumbs, especially in such a neat, tidy house as Miss Barbara Wilkinson's. It was the peas that first attracted the attention of the mousewife to the cage when at last she had time to go up on the window sill. "I have been running here and there and everywhere to get us food," she said, "not allowing myself to come up onto the window sill, and here are these fine white peas, not to mention this piece of fat." (She did not care for the sugar.)

She squeezed through the bars of the cage but, as she was taking the first pea from the tray, the dove moved its wings. I cannot tell you how quickly the mousewife pressed herself back through the bars and jumped down from the sill and ran across the floor and whisked into her hole. It was quicker than a cat can wink its eye. (She thought it was the cat.)

In spite of her great fright she could not help thinking of those peas. She was very hungry. "I had better not go back," she said. "There is something dangerous there," but back she went the very next day.

Soon the dove grew quite used to the mousewife going in and out, and the mouse grew quite used to the dove.

"This is better," said Miss Barbara Wilkinson. "The dove is eating its peas," But, of course, he was not; it was the mouse.

The dove kept his wings folded. The mousewife thought him large and strange and ugly with the speckles on his breast and his fine down. (She thought of it as fur, not feathers.) He was not at all like a mouse; his voice was deep and soft, quite unlike hers, which was a small, high squeaking. Most strange of all, to her, was that he let her take his peas; when she offered them to him he turned his head aside on his breast.

"Then at least take a little water," begged the

mousewife, but he said he did not like water. "Only dew, dew, dew," he said.

"What is dew?" asked the mousewife.

He could not tell her what dew was, but he told her how it shines on the leaves and grass in the early morning for doves to drink. That made him think of night in the woods and of how he and his mate would come down with the first light to walk on the wet earth and peck for food, and of how, then, they would fly over the fields to other woods farther away. He told this to the mousewife too.

"What is fly?" asked the ignorant little mousewife.

"Don't you know?" asked the dove in surprise. He stretched out his wings and they hit the cage bars. Still he struggled to spread them, but the bars were too close, and he sank back on his perch and sank his head on his breast.

The mousewife was strangely moved but she did not know why.

Because he would not eat his peas she brought him crumbs of bread and, once, a preserved blackberry that had fallen from a tart. (But he would not eat the blackberry.) Every day he talked to her about the world outside the window.

He told her of roofs and the tops of trees and of

the rounded shapes of hills and the flat look of fields and of the mountains far away. "But I have never flown as far as that," he said, and he was quiet. He was thinking now he never would.

To cheer him the mousewife asked him to tell her about the wind; she heard it in the house on stormy nights, shaking the doors and windows with more noise than all the mice put together. The dove told her how it blew in the cornfields, making patterns in the corn, and of how it made different sounds in the different sorts of trees, and of how it blew up the clouds and sent them across the sky.

He told her these things as a dove would see them, as it flew, and the mousewife, who was used to creeping, felt her head growing as dizzy as if she were spinning on her tail, but all she said was, "Tell me more."

Each day the dove told her more. When she came he would lift his head and call to her, "Roo coo, roo coo," in his most gentle voice.

"Why do you spend so much time on the window sill?" asked her husband. "I do not like it. The proper place for a mousewife is in her hole or coming out for crumbs and frolic with me."

The mousewife did not answer. She looked far away.

Then, on a happy day, she had a nestful of baby mice. They were not as big as half your thumb, and they were pink and hairless, with pink shut eyes and little pink tails like threads. The mousewife loved them very much. The eldest, who was a girl, she called Flannelette, after the pattern of grey flannel. For several days she thought of nothing and no one else. She was also busy with her husband. His digestion was no better.

One afternoon he went over to the opposite wall to see a friend. He was well enough to do that, he said, but certainly not well enough to go out and look for crumbs. The mice-babies were asleep, the hole was quiet, and the mousewife began to think of the dove. Presently she tucked the nest up carefully and went up on the window sill to see him; also she was hungry and needed some peas.

What a state he was in! He was drooping and nearly exhausted because he had eaten scarcely anything while she had been away. He cowered over her with his wings and kissed her with his beak; she had not known his feathers were so soft or that his breast was so warm. "I thought you had gone, gone, gone," he said over and over again.

The Mousewife 95

"Tut! Tut!" said the mousewife. "A body has other things to do. I can't be always running off to you"; but, though she pretended to scold him, she had a tear at the end of her whisker for the poor dove. (Mouse tears look like millet seeds, which are the smallest seeds I know.)

She stayed a long time with the dove. When she went home, I am sorry to say, her husband bit her on the ear.

That night she lay awake thinking of the dove; mice stay up a great part of the night, but, towards dawn, they, too, curl into their beds and sleep. The mousewife could not sleep. She still thought of the dove. "I cannot visit him as much as I could wish," she said. "There is my husband, and he has never bitten me before. There are the children, and it is surprising how quickly crumbs are eaten up. And no one would believe how dirty a hole can get if it is not attended to every day. But that is not the worst of it. The dove should not be in that cage. It is thoughtless of Miss Barbara Wilkinson." She grew angry as she thought of it. "Not to be able to scamper about the floor! Not to be able to run in and out, or climb up the larder to get at the cheese! Not to flick in and out and to whisk and to feel how you run in your tail! To sit in the trap until your little bones are stiff and your whiskers grow stupid because there is nothing for them to smell or hear or see!" The mousewife could only think of it as a mouse, but she could feel as the dove could feel.

Her husband and Flannelette and the other children were breathing and squeaking happily in their sleep, but the mousewife could hear her heart beating; the beats were little, like the tick of a watch, but they felt loud and disturbing to her. "I cannot sleep," said the mousewife, and then, suddenly, she felt she must go then, that minute, to the dove. "It is too late. He will be asleep," she said, but still she felt she should go.

She crept from her bed and out of the hole onto the floor by the fender. It was bright moonlight, so bright that it made her blink. It was bright as day, but a strange day, that made her head swim and her tail tremble. Her whiskers quivered this way and that, but there was no one and nothing to be seen; no sound, no movement anywhere.

She crept across the pattern of the carpet, stopping here and there on a rose or a leaf or on the scroll of the border. At last she reached the wall and ran lightly up onto the window sill and looked into the cage. In the moonlight she could see the dove sleeping in his feathers, which were ruffled up so that he looked plump and peaceful,

The Mousewife

but, as she watched, he dreamed and called "roo coo" in his sleep and shivered as if he moved. "He is dreaming of scampering and running free," said the mousewife. "Poor thing! Poor dove!"

She looked out into the garden. It too was as bright as day, but the same strange day. She could see the tops of the trees in the wood, and she knew, all at once, that was where the dove should be, in the trees and the garden and the wood.

He called "roo coo" again in his sleep—and she saw that the window was open.

Her whiskers grew still and then they stiffened. She thought of the catch on the cage door. If the catch were pressed down, the door opened.

"I shall open it," said the mousewife. "I shall jump on it and hang from it and swing from it, and it will be pressed down; the door will open and the dove can come out. He can whisk quite out of sight. Miss Barbara Wilkinson will not be able to catch him."

She jumped at the cage and caught the catch in her strong little teeth and swung. The door sprang open, waking the dove.

He was startled and lifted his wings and they hit hard against the cage so that it shivered and the mousewife was almost shaken off.

"Hurry! Hurry!" she said through her teeth.

In a heavy sidelong way he sidled to the door and stood there looking. The mousewife would have given him a push, but she was holding down the catch.

At the door of the cage the dove stretched his neck towards the open window. "Why does he not hurry?" thought the mousewife. "I cannot stay here much longer. My teeth are cracking."

He did not see her or look towards her; then—clap—he took her breath away so that she fell. He had opened his wings and flown straight out. For a moment he dipped as if he would fall, his wings were cramped, and then he moved them and lifted up and up and flew away across the tops of the trees.

The mousewife picked herself up and shook out her bones and her fur.

"So that is to fly," she said. "Now I know." She stood looking out of the window where the dove had gone.

"He has flown," she said. "Now there is no one to tell me about the hills and the corn and the clouds. I shall forget them. How shall I remember when there is no one to tell me and there are so many children and crumbs and bits of fluff to think of?" She had millet tears, not on her whiskers but in her eyes.

"Tut! Tut!" said the mousewife and blinked them away. She looked out again and saw the stars.

It has been given to few mice to see the stars; so rare is it that the mousewife had not even heard of them, and when she saw them shining she thought at first they must be new brass buttons. Then she saw they were very far off, farther than the garden or the wood, beyond the farthest trees. "But not too far for me to see," she said. She knew now that they were not buttons but something far and big and strange. "But not so strange to me," she said, "for I have seen them. And I have seen them for myself," said the mousewife, "without the dove. I can see for myself," said the mousewife, and slowly, proudly, she walked back to bed.

She was back in the hole before her husband waked up, and he did not know that she had been away.

Miss Barbara Wilkinson was astonished to find the cage empty next morning and the dove gone. "Who could have let it out?" asked Miss Wilkinson. She suspected Flora and never knew that she was looking at someone too large and that it was a very small person indeed.

The mousewife is a very old lady mouse now. Her whiskers are grey and she cannot scamper any more; even her running is slow. But her great-great-grandchildren, the children of the children of the children of Flannelette and Flannelette's brothers and sisters, treat her with the utmost respect.

She is a little different from them, though she looks the same. I think she knows something they do not.

ELEMENTS OF SHARED INQUIRY
A Short Course On
Interpretive Reading And Discussion

PART TWO

WRITING GOOD PREPARED QUESTIONS, II

Your prepared questions should be interpretive and you should have some doubt about the answers to them. In addition, your questions should be specific.

Questions that are specific show someone immediately what the problem of interpretation is for you in the story. They are questions that only someone who has read the story carefully could write. Specific questions do not mean questions that take up unimportant details in a story. They should deal with what you consider to be important problems of interpretation. For us, an example of such a question about "The Serpent" would be: Why does the author make it necessary for the birds and fox to be killed in order for the Prince to be saved? We see the question leading to a discussion of many ideas including, Why does the fox kill the birds and then tell the Princess his blood is also needed? and Why is the story written so that the Prince hurts his head when he is flying away?

The trouble with questions that are not specific is that they don't make you think right away about possible answers. Take the question, Why does the story have a happy ending? or, What is the main idea of the story? You could ask these questions about "Cinderella," "Puss-in-Boots" and many other stories you read. Such questions make it hard to think, just as vague directions make it hard to act. Imagine trying to keep a date with a friend who said, "Meet me downtown on Saturday afternoon."

Another quality of prepared questions is that they should

be clear. All good questions should be quickly understood by someone who has read the work. The energy of your fellow participants should be spent in trying to answer interpretive questions, not in trying to figure out what the questions mean. Unclear questions waste time and they can make participants feel stupid. Let's say someone asked this question about "The Serpent": Why is there a multiple change in the hero of the story? the question is confusing and no one will understand the problem. But if you worded the same question clearly—Why does the author have the Prince changed into a serpent and then into a dove?—most participants would be able to start to answer it and would be interested in hearing what the others had to say.

EXERCISE 6

"The Serpent"

Many of the questions in this exercise are not good questions because they do not have one or more of the qualities we described today and at your last session. You decide which statement below best describes each question and then place the appropriate letter next to it.

      A) Question is not clear

      B) Question is not specific enough

      C) No doubt about the answer to the question

      D) Question is not answerable from the story

      E) Question is satisfactory

_____ 1. Why is there magic in the story?

_____ 2. Will the ogress who changed the Prince into a serpent be punished?

_____ 3. Is the duplicity of Grannonia justified in terms of its consequences?

_____ 4. Why is there an unhappy situation at the beginning of the story?

_____ 5. Why does the gardener have to perform some action before the serpent can carry out the King's request?

_____ 6. Are Grannonia and the Prince loyal to each other?

_____ 7. Does a serpent often turn out to be an evil character in stories?

_____ 8. Did the King believe the serpent would be able to meet all the conditions he set for marrying Grannonia?

_____ 9. Is the appropriateness of punishment secondary to the happy ending?

_____10. Why does the cure for the Prince require the blood of the fox and the birds?

STUDYING A PASSAGE IN A STORY

Even is you have a good memory, you have probably found it necessary during a discussion to read some passage again either to answer a question about it or to decide whether someone else's answer is correct. These are good reasons for always having the story you are discussing right in front of you. Another is that having the story there gives you a chance to do a very close reading of a passage. By a close reading, we mean trying to guess what the author is trying to make us think or feel *line by line and sometimes word by word*. Sometimes, this is a useful way to get discussion started when no one has understood a story very well.

The first step is to find a passage that you want to look at closely and then have someone in the group read it aloud. Even if it is difficult, you may get some new sense of what it is about from hearing it read aloud.

Then go over the passage, line by line. Ask *any* questions that you can think of about the meaning of words, phrases, and sentences. If you are called on to answer a question that someone else has, try to put your response into your own words instead of using the words of the author. Feel free to turn to other sections of the work that you think will help you answer questions about the passage you are reading closely.

It may help to start by finding out who is talking in the passage. It may be the author speaking to you directly or through a narrator, or one character speaking to another character. Also, try to get a rough idea of where you are in the story. Look briefly at the page or two before the passage to help refresh your memory.

Studying a Passage in a Story

EXERCISE 7

"Prince Rabbit"

To show you how textual analysis works, see how many questions you can ask and answer for the following passage from "Prince Rabbit." We have suggested a few questions. Try to think of others, too.

"There is no doubt that the Rabbit has won," said the Chancellor.

"Which rabbit?" cried the King crossly. "They're both rabbits."

"The one with the white spots behind the ears," said Rabbit helpfully. "May I get down?"

There was a sudden cry from the back of the hall. "Your Majesty?"

"Well, well, what is it?"

The enchanter pushed his way forward. "May I look, Your Majesty?" he said in a trembling voice. "White spots behind the ears? Dear, dear! Allow me!" He seized Rabbit's ears and bent them this way and that.

"Ow!" said Rabbit.

"It is! Your Majesty, it is!"

"Is what?"

Studying a Passage in a Story

"The son of the late King Nicodemus, whose country is now joined to your own. Prince Silvio."

1. What kind of contest has the Rabbit just won?

2. Why does the King say "Which rabbit?" crossly?

3. Why does the author write the story so that Lord Calomel is turned into a rabbit for the last contest?

4. Why was the last contest one that a human being would ordinarily be more likely to win?

5. Why does the author have Lord Calomel compete as a man in the other contests?

6. Why does the author have the Rabbit win the last contest?

7. Why does the Rabbit turn out to be an enchanted prince?

8. Did the author want you to guess earlier in the story that the Rabbit was the enchanted prince?

9. If so, why weren't we told earlier about the white spots behind the ears?

QUESTIONS THAT CONNECT TWO STORIES

For some of your Junior Great Books discussions, we have selected two stories instead of one. For example, at an earlier meeting you may have done "Cinderella" and "Tattercoats." In reading two selections for a meeting, you may find yourself thinking about the ways two stories are alike and different. For instance, after reading "The Foolish Man" and "The Water of Life," we would like to discuss the question: Why does the trusting nature of the foolish man result in his being eaten up when the trusting nature of the youngest son results in his gaining the king's favor and the princess?

There can be advantages in asking questions that relate one story to another. Discovering connections between stories can result in new ideas about the meaning of each story. For example, in answering the question we just asked, you might start to think about whether God approved of the foolish man's complaining. You might also begin to consider the importance of the deeds that the youngest son performs in "The Water of Life."

Questions that try to relate one story to another should have all the qualities of good prepared questions. They should be interpretive questions, you should have some doubt about the answer, and you should believe that they can be answered from the story. They should also be specific and clear.

For the next meeting, try to write a few interpretive questions that relate "The Fire on the Mountain" and "Janot

Cooks for the Emperor." Your questions may take up ways in which the stories are alike or different.

EXERCISE 9

"The Fire on the Mountain"
and
"Janot Cooks for the Emperor"

Place an (R) next to each question that *specifically* relates "The Fire on the Mountain" to "Janot Cooks for the Emperor."

_____ 1. Why do both Haptom and the Emperor realize that they lost the bet only after they are placed in situations like those their servants were in on the mountain top?

_____ 2. Why do Haptom and the Emperor have to be placed in uncomfortable situations before they realize they were wrong?

_____ 3. Why do both stories deal with a conflict?

_____ 4. In what ways are the characters in both stories alike and different?

_____ 5. Why does the author of "The Fire on the Mountain" have Arha need help in knowing what to do, while the author of "Janot Cooks for the Emperor" has Janot depend on himself?

_____ 6. Do both authors have the same attitude toward their characters?

_____ 7. In both stories, why do both men risk their lives to obtain farms rather than money?

____ 8. Which story did you like best?

____ 9. Why do both stories end the way they do?

____10. Why does Janot, unlike Arha, keep insisting it isn't cold on the mountain?

SOLVING THE PROBLEM IN SHARED INQUIRY

Interpretive questions can usually be answered satisfactorily in more than one way, so there is no one *right* answer in shared inquiry. In shared inquiry, the solution to an interpretive problem is that point in a discussion when all the members of your group could, if called upon: (1) answer the interpretive question on which the discussion is based in their own way; and (2) support their answers with facts from the selection.

You can see from this definition that solving a problem does not mean that everyone has to agree on one answer or that even most of the group must think a particular answer is correct. You have a solution *when you are convinced that the way in which you answer an interpretive question can be supported with facts that satisfy you.* Even if everyone else is satisfied with an answer, you should feel free to bring up points about an interpretive question as long as you have any doubt about how *you* would answer it.

One sign that the group is leaving an interpretive question before everyone has answered it to his or her satisfaction is that participants still want to talk about the question even after the leaders have switched to another question. If that happens, your discussion leaders should backtrack for a moment or two to find out whether new facts or ideas are being raised that could provide another answer to the question you were discussing earlier.

There are also signs to show that you have said about as much as you can in answer to an interpretive question: the group begins to repeat itself, to take up minor points, and to wander away from the question. When that happens, the group has probably run out of ideas in answer to the question, and it is time to switch to a new one.

EXERCISE 10

"The Mousewife"

The purpose of this exercise is to illustrate what we mean by resolution and to test our statement that resolution of an interpretive question will be different for different groups. Your discussion leaders will divide you into two or three small groups and ask a member of each group to list all the topics or ideas you would have to discuss to answer the question:

What is the Mousewife looking for that the dove gives her?